The Hard
Detective

ALSO BY H. R. F. KEATING

The Hard Detective

H. R. F. Keating

St. Martin's Minotaur New York

ISBN 0-312-24648-X

First published in Great Britain by Macmillan Publishers Ltd

First St. Martin's Minotaur Edition: May 2000

10 9 8 7 6 5 4 3 2 1

Chapter One

'We rang the bell, right?'

Detective Chief Inspector Harriet Martens pointed, finger held two inches away, to the untouched dusty plastic bellpush.

'We rang the bell,' murmuring, keyed-up voices echoed.

'We got no answer.'

'We got no answer.'

The subdued echo laced now with suppressed laughter.

'We had reason to believe evidence might be being destroyed.'

'Evidence. Destroyed.'

Tension held for one half-second.

Then . . .

'Right. Go, go, go.'

The four constables with the ram, already swung well back, took one long concerted pace forward and brought it hurtling towards the door. It struck with a single solid thud just beside the lock. The scratched and scarred, badly painted wood cracked in a sharp explosion and the door flew back.

'Hole in one.'

But Harriet hardly heard the shout of triumph as she led the raiding party in. Up the narrow stairs in front of her, two at a time, and straight for the door of the back bedroom where surveillance had placed Terry Dunne, persistent burglar.

A bleary shout of rage and questioning came from inside as she yanked at the knob and flung the door wide. Terry, hairy-chested, face thickly beard-shadowed, reared up in the bed, glaring.

'Okay, Terry, you're nicked.'

Sergeant Metcalf, Harriet's Number Two on the raid, gave a wide grin.

'Another scrote hauled in on the great B Division *Stop the Rot* campaign,' he proclaimed.

'Only one,' Harriet shot back as she switched her silenced mobile back on. 'I want another half-dozen seen to before this day's out. Never mind what for. Anything that breaks any law. Jump on them. Jump on them. It's the only way to—'

But the woman on the other side of the frowsy bed, who had tumbled out and was standing there, body dead-white in the dawn light, burst out now with a stream of abuse, strident voice filling the whole cluttered, sour-smelling room.

'What the fuck d'you mean breaking in here? Christ, sodding police. Where d'you think this is then? Fucking Nazi Germany? Fucking well get out, won't you. Leering sodding bastards. Why, don't—'

But Harriet had taken three sharp paces to put herself in front of the screeching girl, face hardly more than an inch away.

'Shut up.'

The stream of abuse stopped. Abruptly as if an iron shutter had clanged down.

Harriet turned to the squad clustered at the door.

'All right, get on with it. Take the place apart. Sergeant Metcalf will note each find as it's made, and don't fail to account for every—'

Her mobile rang.

She turned to take the call.

For two minutes she listened in silence to the jabbering voice at her ear.

'Right,' she said when it ceased. 'I'll come.'

She turned back to Metcalf, clipping handcuffs on now roughly dressed Terry Dunne, not without a savage grin as he twisted his wrists behind his back.

'Someone's knifed a night-patrol constable. PC Titmuss. Body's been found somewhere just off New Street. So much for me coming out at the sharp end with you lot. Take over, Sergeant, will you? Give Terry the full rights spiel.'

With the formula words rattling out behind her, she hurried off.

'Terry Dunne, I am arresting you on suspicion of burglary. You do not have to say anything. But it may harm your defence if you do not mention when questioned something which you later rely on in court. Anything you do say . . .'

She was pleased, as she brought her car to a halt behind a Greater Birchester Police van, to see that already efficient steps had been taken to secure the scene. Blue plastic tapes were in place, and a woman constable had been posted at the far end of the street to re-direct early-morning traffic. But, as it had been Inspector Roberts who, passing by, had found the body and called her at Terry Dunne's, she expected no less. Rob Roberts might be the sort of man who was happiest poring over the Personnel files he was in charge of at Headquarters but he knew his business.

'Rob,' she greeted him as, dressed only in jeans, trainers and a thick high-necked white jersey, he came forward. 'Put me in the picture. Was he dead when you found him? And what are you doing down here anyway?'

Round ruddy face, thatch of fair hair sticking up unbrushed, generous fair moustache, wide blue eyes, he grinned. A little sheepishly.

'I was out for a walk. Can't stay asleep all that long, these days. So I often come down here and get myself an early paper.'

'And as you passed you saw . . . what?'

'Come and look. The doc hasn't arrived yet. The body's still where it was when I noticed something at the entrance to that passageway.'

The alleyway was so narrow it was still all but pitch-dark inside despite the slowly gathering March day-light. PC Titmuss lay face-down, with his helmet, which had not fallen from his head, protruding by two or three inches on to the street itself. At the side of his neck towards the back, just above the collar of his dark-blue greatcoat, there was what was almost certainly a deep knife wound. It had sent a dark runnel of blood on to the greasy paving stones below.

Harriet stood in silence, carefully looking at the area immediately round the body's slumped blue mass.

'Fag-ends in plenty,' she said. 'Place doesn't look as if a road sweeper ever comes near it. You know what? I think young Titmuss used to step inside here every night and give himself a crafty smoke. Bloody lucky I never caught him at it.'

'Oh, come on,' Rob Roberts answered. 'We've all done that, or something like it, in our early days on the beat, haven't we? Only natural really.'

'No, Rob, we haven't all done it. And we shouldn't any of us have done it, or be doing it now. No one's as alert as they ought to be if they're sneaking a quick fag, and you know it.'

Rob Roberts sighed.

'Well, some of us don't match up to your high standards,' he said, adding a half-murmured *ma'am* to counter what might be thought impertinence to a senior officer, even if one half a dozen years younger than himself.

'Scenes-of-Crime should be here by now,' Harriet said by way of closing the subject.

'Yes. I called Headquarters soon as I'd spoken to you.'

'Wrong order, Rob.'

'Well, I thought as he was one of ours . . .'

'I dare say. But evidence has to be the number one priority. All the more so when the victim wears the cloth. Who do you think went for him like that? What do you know about him?'

'Not all that much, as a matter of fact. I don't think I've had his file out more than once a year, if that.

This may have been just the result of some chance encounter.'

'Stabbed in the back like that? A chance encounter? I don't think so. No, someone almost certainly was waiting for him, hiding there in the dark. Where does the passageway go, do you know?'

'It doesn't go anywhere now, actually. It's just a dead-end. By daylight you can see that. It probably used to run between two buildings here. But a lot of the old offices were torn down back in the fifties, and I imagine this little space just got left. Why it never gets swept, I dare say.'

'And why Titmuss thought it a nice place for a smoke. And why someone knew it was a good spot to wait for him down at the dark end. You don't know anything about Titmuss's private life, you said?'

'There'll be the basics in his file. Next-of-kin, date of birth. I'll look it up soon as I get the chance, but I'm pretty sure he wasn't married.'

'Involved with any of the enemy? He wouldn't be the first. Owing gambling money?'

'I couldn't say.'

It was an unspoken, tight-lipped rebuke.

'Just because he's dead, Inspector,' Harriet answered sharply, 'it doesn't mean he was incapable of doing things he oughtn't to when he was alive. But if you do know nothing to his detriment, you know nothing. We'll have to— Ah, Scenes-of-Crime. And about time.'

She turned away to where behind her own car the big white Scenes-of-Crime van was pulling up. But, as she did so, something at the police tape at the opposite end of the protected area caught her eye.

'Isn't that the fellow from the *Evening Star*?' she said. 'Crime reporter. What's his name? Patterson. Tim Patterson. Who the hell told him about this? Somebody's going to be in a whole lot of trouble before very long. And he's talking to that WPC there. It's the little Muslim one, isn't it?'

'WPC Syed,' Rob Roberts said, with what sounded like quick defensiveness. 'Rukshana Syed. Probationer. Useful addition to the Force.'

'Well, she won't be any sort of addition to the Force much longer if she goes on chatting to *Evening Star* reporters.'

She strode, a swooping lioness, down to the far tape.

'You, Mr Patterson. What are you doing distracting one of my officers from her duty? We don't need the press here. There'll be a statement in due course.'

'DCI Martens,' the young reporter, pale-faced, lank-haired, beaky nose actually twitching, eyes behind big glasses flicking and flicking, came back at her, 'am I right in thinking one of your officers has been killed? Is it murder? How did it happen? Was he making an arrest? Was he carrying out your personal orders to check any and every sort of wrong behaviour? Have we got a killing here as a direct result of your *Stop the Rot* campaign?'

'I said there'll be a statement when we're ready to put one out. Now, unless you want to get arrested, move on.'

For a moment he stood there, patently wondering if he could risk yet another provocative question. But then he turned on his heel and walked rapidly back to his car further down the street.

'Right, Constable Syed,' Harriet snapped out. 'Do you know who I am?'

The ferocity of the question turned the young Muslim girl's face momentarily pale.

'Yes. Yes,' she stammered out. 'You're DCI Martens.'

'*Yes? Yes?* Haven't you learnt yet how to address a senior officer?'

'Yes. I mean, yes, ma'am.'

'That's better. Now, what were you doing talking to that man?'

'I— I— er. He just asked me a question. Er— ma'am. So I answered.'

'He just asked you a question. Didn't you know he was a reporter?'

'No. No, ma'am, I had no idea.'

'Well, you ought to have done. When you're out on the street you ought to know about every damn thing you see. Which building is which. Which street goes where. What everyone you come across is doing there. Do you understand what harm talking to someone from the press about a murder case can cause? Well, do you?'

'I— I'm not sure, ma'am.'

'Well, you ought to be. It's the duty of every officer who knows anything at all about a murder to keep that information strictly to themselves. That way we'll have some hope of catching the man who's killed one of your fellow officers. Of catching him when he comes out with something he shouldn't know about. Unless some stupid little girl has already gone and blurted it out to a reporter. Understand?'

'Yes, ma'am. I'm sorry, ma'am. I just . . .'

In the pale early morning light it was just possible to see a tear brimming up in the Muslim girl's eye.

'Well, in future, Constable, *just* don't. You're on probation in this Force, so let me tell you if I get to hear of one single other piece of stupidity like this, you'll be out. Out.'

'Yes, ma'am.'

Harriet swung away and went over to where the Scenes-of-Crime team were unloading their gear and getting clumsily into their bulky white coveralls and big plastic shoe-protectors.

'Morning, ma'am,' the sergeant in charge said. 'Is it right it's Titty Titmuss who's caught it?'

'It is, Sergeant. One of our own. So I want every piece of evidence, possible and impossible, found and bagged and handed to Forensic. And where's Inspector Palfrey? Scenes-of-Crime is his unit: he should be here.'

'On his way, ma'am,' the sergeant replied, doing his best to sound as if he was speaking the truth.

'Well, when he gets here – if he does – tell him if any man or woman in his team misses one tiny thing and loses us the bastard who did this, then he'll be answering to me.'

'You can rely on us, ma'am. But Titty Titmuss . . . He may have been a pretty poor copper but he didn't deserve this.'

'A poor copper, Sergeant? What do you mean?'

The sergeant looked abashed.

'Well, I shouldn't really have spoken ill of the dead,' he said.

'Ill of the dead? Let me tell you, Sergeant, if you

know anything about PC Titmuss, ill or good, it's your duty to cough it up.'

'Yes, ma'am. Well, it's not really all that much. But Titty was a bit of a skiver, you know. Well, not to put too fine a point on it, he was one hell of a skiver. I mean, if he could get out of doing anything, he would, and, if he couldn't get out of it, he'd do just as little as he could manage. I suppose, because of that he's been— That is, he was put on night patrol for almost the whole of the past month. As I understand it. Only canteen gossip, of course.'

'Yes. Well, thank you, Sergeant. I'll check on that. If Titmuss was coming every night at much the same time to stand and smoke in that nice little dark corner over there, then someone will have known about it. And that someone is the one we're going to put where he belongs. In prison for the rest of his damn life.'

Chapter Two

Seeing that everything was up and running, Harriet began to think of heading for home to grab some breakfast and change – white blouse, grey barathea skirt – before getting to her office to direct inquiries. On the point of leaving, a spatter of rain flicked down and she noticed Inspector Roberts looking up apprehensively at the mass of dark cloud overhead.

'Inspector. Want a lift as far as my house? You'll get soaked in that jersey.'

He came over at a trot.

'Thank you, ma'am. That'd be a great help. But I didn't know you realized I lived not so far from you.'

'A detective can never know enough, Inspector.'

'Well, I'm glad you know what you do about me. I'd be wet through walking back in this. Still, it should be well over before we reach your place. Almost into April showers time now.'

In that Rob Roberts was wrong. When they pulled up outside Harriet's house the rain was coming down a lot harder.

'Look,' she said, 'I can't really spare the time to take you round to Meadow Avenue. I'll have a hell of a lot to see to at the nick. But I could lend you my husband's gardening mac. He's away working in Brazil. It's pretty ropey but it'll keep out the wet.'

'That's very kind.' Rob Roberts paused a moment. 'Mrs Piddock.'

Harriet looked at him.

'So, even though you're not a detective, you know something about me I prefer to keep under wraps.'

'Heading up Personnel, I have my sources.'

'Right. But don't go broadcasting my married name everywhere. It suits me at work to use the name I had when I joined the Force. Keeps my private life private.'

'Oh. No, no, of course I won't.'

'Right. Well, you can keep out of the rain under the porch while I fetch the coat. I can't let you in. Been getting some nasty presents through the letter-box from the local layabouts since *Stop the Rot* got going. Shit, dog and human, and liable to go all over the carpet when I swing the door back.'

'But— Well, with respect, ma'am, shouldn't you be having some protection?'

'Against parcels of shit? I don't think so. Up to now it's only the riff-raff roundabout hitting back – the louts who sell drugs at the corner, urinators after dark, kids shining laser pens in people's eyes, the casual vandals. All the ones I've been having taught lessons.'

She looked across to the sturdy veranda-like porch that gave the house its touch of character.

'You'll be dry under there.'

'I'll be fine,' Rob Roberts said. 'And thanks for thinking of the coat. I'll bring it back one evening, if that's all right.'

'Whenever . . . Oh, and one thing more . . . If there

does turn out to be anything other than the bare facts in your files about PC Titmuss, remember I want to know. There must be some reason why he was killed. Anything that gives me even a hint could help.'

'Understood, ma'am.'

They pelted then through the downpour to the porch. Up on its low platform Rob Roberts gave an apologetic cough.

'Excuse me, ma'am, but what about the really big boys? Before long won't one of them think of leaving something worse than dog-shit in your letter-box? A bomb, even?'

'Frankly, Rob, I wouldn't be sorry if they did. It'd show that the real criminals hate me. And, as I hate them equally, that'd be satisfying rather than worrying.'

Rob Roberts sighed.

'An eye for an eye,' he said. 'Rather you than me.'

'An eye for an eye? Something from the Bible, if I remember my Religious Studies at school. But, yes, I think I like it. An eye for an eye. Yes.'

'Well, it's actually *Life for life, eye for eye, tooth for tooth, hand for hand, foot for foot, burning for burning, wound for wound, stripe for stripe*. Exodus, twenty-one, verse twenty-three. Had that drummed into me in Sunday School. Bit different, I imagine, from what you used to be taught.'

'So you know even more about me than my married name?'

'I suppose I do. When you began getting into the news, I looked up your file. St Anne's School. Cambridge University. High-flyers course at Bramshill . . .'

'We'll see about the high flying. If I make a mess of

this investigation, it'll be damn low flying for the rest of my career.'

'You won't make a mess of it, ma'am. If anyone can find the bloke who stabbed Titty Titmuss, it'll be you.'

But, once again, Rob Roberts turned out not to be right. Before her busy day was over Harriet had a call in her office at Queen Street, B Division headquarters, from the Chief Constable's staff officer and then from Sir Michael himself.

'DCI Martens?'

'Sir?'

'The Titmuss murder. I understand your investigation's fully under way.'

'I hope it is, sir. Incident Room set up, door-to-door reports beginning to come in. And everything, of course, logged into the HOLMES computer.'

'No, DCI.'

'No, sir?'

'No, you will find now that you are no longer logged into HOLMES.'

'But— But, sir—'

'Now, I don't want you to misunderstand this, Miss Martens. But the fact of the matter is that, after a good deal of consideration, I have given the inquiry to Detective Superintendent Froggott. No reflection on you. But the murder of a police officer must get absolutely one hundred per cent priority, nor do I want your *Stop the Rot* campaign to lose momentum. You know that has my full backing. My very fullest. All the press comment it's attracted does nothing but good for the image of

Greater Birchester Police. And Froggott's a first-class detective, as you'll know. As you'll know. He left your B Division in a very healthy state. Fine clear-up rate.'

For a moment some bitter thoughts ran through Harriet's head. Yes, Froggy Froggott had achieved a high clear-up rate. But as much by cases *Taken into Consideration* as by cases brought to a proper result. Easy enough to be able to record impressive figures by persuading criminals already caught for one crime to admit to a string of others in the hope of leniency. But that was not putting untouched criminals where they should be. Behind bars. First-class detective Froggy Froggott may get called, but to anyone who's served under him and has eyes in their head he's a first-class blusterer.

His favourite trick came into her mind, together with the evil yellow-toothed grin on his jowly red face as he produced it: the junior officer foolish enough to wish him good morning and his invariable reply *I don't want a weather report: I want action.*

Action Froggy loved. He was never happier than leading some major operation from the front. With the prospect of parading his hard image to the TV cameras, or in getting some banging quotes into the sensation-mongering *Evening Star* if he was less lucky. But, she told herself, that hard line was no more than an image, something for the cameras or the minds of the more easily impressed among the lower ranks of Greater Birchester Police. Froggy, damn him, was hard for the sake of being hard. Hard so as to gloss up the picture which he devoted himself to creating, the Hard Detective.

15

And where does that leave me? Where does it leave the detective chief inspector the local media have been busy of late building up into another Hard Detective, and one with the extra frisson of being a woman?

Well, blast them all, I don't make myself hard for the image it creates. I make myself hard because it's necessary. There are villains in the world, nasty men, hard men – and, yes, hard, nasty women, too – and they have to be met with an equal hardness. A more than equal hardness. All right, not every offender is a through-and-through hard man. But even the small fry do their daily best to cultivate the fuck-you side of themselves. And need putting down just as much as the bigger fish, if the world, or my part of Birchester at least, is to be made habitable.

That's what I'm here for. Whether at the beginning I liked it or not. Whether in the beginning I even knew that this was to be my lot, my place in the scheme of things.

But now it is. And I am. And that's all there is to it.

She pulled herself back into paying the distant, tinny voice of the Chief Constable some attention.

'Yes, sir,' she said at last. 'I quite understand your decision. And, yes, it will leave my hands free to do some proper policing in the Division.'

Then, in case she had allowed herself to go a little far in hinting about the slack state Froggy Froggott had left behind him when he had been given the city's prestigious A Division, she quickly added: 'No one could be better than Mr Froggott, sir, at getting a result. And you can rest assured I'll give him maximum co-operation.'

She got her opportunity to fulfil that promise within an hour of the Chief Constable's call. Her phone rang.

'DCI Martens here.'

'Scenes-of-Crime, ma'am. Sergeant Bolton. Thought you'd like to know direct what results we got at New Street. Nothing from the ground, no bootmarks, nothing like that. That heavy shower coming on so sudden washed the whole area clean before we could even get it covered over. Some bits of rubbish right at the far end, but nothing that looks as if it'll be at all helpful. And of course the body's gone to the pathologist. But there was one thing we did find . . .'

Harriet knew she should have said at this first opportunity that the investigation was now Superintendent Froggott's. But she could not resist putting in a quick 'Well?'

'Little thread of wool caught on an old piece of ironwork jutting out of the wall. Just where someone darting forward in that narrow space would have brushed against it. Can't have been there long, the thread, still good and fluffy. It's gone to Forensic, of course. But I bet my bottom dollar I know what it is.'

And again 'Well?'

'From a royal-blue donkey jacket, ma'am. I ought to know. Used to have one just like it myself. It won't exactly help find the fellow, but, when we do, if we get hold of that coat of his it'll be absolutely good enough for the court. It'll be bloodstained, almost for a cert.'

'Good work, Sergeant. But I have to tell you something. The whole investigation has been handed to Detective Superintendent Froggott at A Division. So he's the one you should be talking to.'

'Oh.'

Long pause.

'But, ma'am . . . Well, I mean, why's that, if I may ask? Body firmly in B Div's territory.'

'Comes from the top, Sergeant. The Chief's decision.'

'Well, yes, then. I suppose he knows best. But— Well . . .'

'Yes?'

Another silence. Then a burst of candour.

'Ma'am, I suppose you couldn't pass the info on to Mr Froggott yourself? Er— Well, look, the truth is I got on the wrong side of him once, and— And, well, he's not inclined to pay much attention to anything I say.'

Harriet smiled into the safe blankness of the phone.

'It's not exactly correct procedure, Sergeant,' she said, her voice determinedly neutral. 'But if, as you say, you'd find it difficult to give this information to Mr Froggott in a way that makes sure he sees its importance, I could pass it on. Something like this shouldn't be left tucked away in the computer until someone happens to notice it.'

'Thank you, ma'am. It's what you might call a weight off my mind.'

Harriet got through to Detective Superintendent Froggott right away. What you don't like doing should be done at once.

'Yes, Miss Martens? How can I help a lady?'

She saw at once his leering face, surmounting bristle of grey hair, big yellowy teeth bared in a self-delighted grin. But she had coped with his sort of heavy irony often enough in the past.

'I have a message from Scenes-of-Crime about PC Titmuss, sir,' she answered, dead-pan. 'Sent to me in error. They apparently hadn't realized the investigation is with you.'

'Just like them. Lazy swines, always were. And none of their bits and bobs much good to anyone, ask me.'

'Yes, sir. But, if this is what it seems to be, I think this time they may have done the investigation some good.'

'For me to judge, Miss.'

Call me Miss just once more, and . . .

'Of course, sir. It's just that they found a strand of cloth at the murder scene, and it looks very much as if it can't have been there before last night.'

'A strand of cloth? Well, thanks for telling me. Now I'll have the killer locked up in no time at all.'

'Well, no, sir. But Scenes-of-Crime seem pretty certain that the thread – it's royal-blue wool – comes from a donkey jacket.'

'A donkey jacket. And I suppose now you want me to arrest every man in however many millions there are in Birchester who's ever owned a donkey jacket.'

'No, sir.'

Play it strictly cool.

'It's just that Scenes-of-Crime are pretty well convinced that when you do get your man, if you can get hold of his jacket, there should be a hundred per cent match.'

'First catch your bloody hare. Well, Mrs Beeton, thank you for your information. And tell Scenes-of-Crime that I have set up my Incident Room, that I do know how to run an investigation, and that, if they've found something they think is a vital clue, they know where to log it. Right?'

'Yes, sir. Only . . . Well, I do think a donkey jacket does tell us something.'

'Oh, yes. And what's that, Shirley Holmes?'

'Just that it is definitely a man we're looking for, sir.'

'A man? A man? Who else do you think I'm looking for? You're not trying to make me think it could be a woman who upped and stuck a knife into one of my constables? Let me tell you, I remember young Titmuss from when I was running B Div, and he wasn't the sort of lad that would let a woman stick a knife in him. If anything he'd be sticking something in a woman, and it wouldn't be cold steel.'

'No, sir.'

She put the phone down before she said anything more. She had told him what she had been asked to – tough nut or no tough nut – and now her conscience could be clear. And, besides, unlikely though it was, a woman could conceivably have used that knife. Sharp enough by the look of the wound, and not a great deal of force needed. She could even have deliberately dressed in a sombre, concealing donkey jacket.

Well, back to making B Division's territory as unpleasant as possible for the enemy. Back to infusing every officer in the Division with the will to enforce *Stop the Rot* twenty-four hours a day, whether pulling up a youth who's dropped his fish-and-chips paper or by putting observation on the next break-in merchant after Terry Dunne.

However, it seemed she was not free of the murder

of PC Titmuss yet. Before she had gone off-duty the woman detective sergeant in charge of the station Rape Centre came in. She had realised, she said, that the crime in the case she was dealing with at the moment had been committed in the very dead-end passageway off New Street where later that night PC Titmuss had been stabbed. Her victim, who had only now brought herself to report what had happened, had stated that the evening before at the pub she had suddenly found herself in a sort of trance and a boy who had been chatting her up had led her, under the pretence of seeing her to her bus, to the passageway where he had without much fuss raped her.

'It could be, ma'am,' Sergeant Grant said, 'that traces of my victim's ordeal will have affected the later Scenes-of-Crime search. But I don't know if it's really worth reporting. It wasn't the sort of rape to leave many clues. I'm pretty sure the girl was slipped a Rohypnol tablet, a Roofie, in the rum-and-Coke that nasty little tyke kindly bought her. They're tasteless, you know. And make a victim putty in anyone's hands inside thirty minutes. God knows, using them's a trick being played more and more these days. You can buy them under the table in a pub for as little as three quid.'

Harriet, inwardly cursing, told her that, yes, she should report the circumstances to Superintendent Froggott. She was not going to let Froggy have the least excuse to berate any of her officers.

But at last her day was over. Or so she thought.

She had just got home and was beginning to get herself some supper when the phone rang. Never sure whether a call would be for DCI Martens or for Mrs

21

John Piddock, mother of twin sons occasionally remembering to ring from university, she had developed the habit of answering simply with her number.

'Chief Inspector Martens?'

'Yes?'

'Duty sergeant here, ma'am. Some bad news, I'm afraid.'

Terry Dunne escaped somehow? Raped girl refusing to give evidence after all? Yet another bad break-in?

'Yes, Sergeant?'

'It's WPC Syed, ma'am.'

'Yes. I know her. Well?'

'She's been killed, ma'am, I'm sorry to say.'

For an instant, with the idea still near the surface of her mind of PC Titmuss and that knife in his neck, she thought that Rukshana Syed must have been killed in the same way. But then the implication of the sergeant's *I'm sorry to say* struck home. He would hardly have added those words if the young Muslim probationer had been murdered. So . . . an accident of some sort.

'What happened, Sergeant?'

'It seems she was on her way home, ma'am – she lives with her boyfriend in a flat just off Victoria Road – and rides home by bike. Well, she'd just got to the other end of Queen Street, where the traffic flow's heaviest with vehicles from Market Place joining in, when she swerved or fell for some reason and went right under a No 14 bus. Nothing the driver could do about it, so the constable who was there said.'

'Jesus, poor kid. Only this morning I was giving her a bollocking for talking to a reporter down where PC Titmuss was killed, and now . . .'

'You're not saying there's a connection with the Titmuss killing, ma'am?'

'No, no. Of course not. There's nothing to indicate this was anything but an accident, is there?'

'Not so far as I know, ma'am. PC Wilkinson who attended is here now if you want to see him.'

'Yes. I'll come straight in.'

Wilkinson, a man in his early twenties, was sitting alone in the station canteen, his helmet on the table in front of him. It was plain that he had not had to deal with many road deaths before. His long gaunt face was still pale and he was clutching a cup of tea with both hands as if to stop them trembling. He stood up as Harriet approached but, when she told him to sit, did so with rapidity.

'Did you know WPC Syed?' she asked.

'No, ma'am. Well, only by sight if you know what I mean.'

'All right then. If she wasn't a friend, you'd better make an effort to pull yourself together. This won't be the last fatal you'll have to attend.'

Her brusque words brought a flare of resentment to his eyes.

'I know it's unpleasant,' she said sharply. 'But a police officer has to be ready for unpleasantness. The trick is: tell yourself you're just going to get on with what you've got to do, and then do it. If you ever get into CID you'll need to learn that, when you attend a post-mortem and have to see a dead body's guts being pulled out on to the dissecting table. But that has to be done, and some police officer has to watch.'

'Yes, ma'am.'

'Right then. Stop feeling sorry for yourself, and tell me all you know about this accident. There'll be an inquest, and you'll have to give evidence as well as the traffic patrol. So you need to have every circumstance clear in your mind. Were you directly at the scene when it happened?'

'No, ma'am, not quite. I'd just gone off-duty and was walking down Queen Street.'

'All right. So you were close by?'

'Well, yes, ma'am. I heard some woman scream, and I turned to look back. I saw that bus, a No 14, sort of slewed half across the roadway and I guessed what must have occurred.'

'So, then . . .?'

'I made my way back there, ma'am, and I saw Ruk-what-do-they-call-her—'

'You saw Syed, yes?'

'Well, she was still half under the bus. And it was plain she was dead. She'd gone right under the nearside wheel, with her bike all mangled up beneath her.'

PC Wilkinson showed signs of falling back into the state of shock he had been in when she had gone over to him.

'You're certain from your own observations that the bus driver couldn't have avoided her?'

'Yes, ma'am.'

'And you've noted that in your pocket-book? Yes?'

A slow dense blush came up on the long gaunt face in front of her.

'Well, no. No, ma'am. I— I hadn't got round to that yet.'

'Then you better had, Constable. Now. Recollections long after the event are hardly worth having. So, out with your book here and now. What time was it when you attended the accident? Write it down.'

'Er— I don't know, ma'am. I mean, it must have been about . . . Well, we both of us had just gone off-duty. I saw her getting her bike as I came out. So . . . So I suppose it was, say, ten or fifteen minutes past six.'

'When you next have to deal with an RTA, Constable, take a look at your watch first of all. Good evidence is always needed at any road accident.'

'Yes, ma'am.'

'Right. So what else besides the body and the bicycle and the position of the bus did you notice? You took the driver's name and number, I suppose? And the conductor's?'

'Conductress, as a matter of fact, ma'am. But she didn't see anything. She says.'

'And other witnesses? Did you get any other names?'

'Well, no, ma'am. I'm afraid by the time I'd looked to see if Ruk— To see if WPC Syed could possibly still be alive everybody there at the time seemed to have buggered off. Not wanting to be caught up in it, I suppose. And then Traffic arrived and took over. I don't know if they found any witnesses.'

'Well, we'll see. So, was there anything else you saw

25

that you should be putting in your pocket-book this moment?'

'No, ma'am. No, I don't think so. Well, there was one thing that struck me, though. Sort of funny really.'

'I take it you mean *odd* rather than *hilarious*?'

'Yes. Yes, ma'am. Sorry, it sort of slipped out because it was fun— I mean very kind of odd.'

'Well, what was this odd circumstance?'

'It was just . . . Well, just where it happened, on the kerb there, looking like it was deliberately pointing at the bike and— And, well, the body, someone had put down what I thought at first was a pen, a big, red, old-fashioned fountain-pen. But when I took a closer look – I don't really know why, except it seemed somehow as if it had been placed there on purpose – I saw it was one of those what-you-call-'ems. Laser pens. I wouldn't of known what it was only I took one like it off a couple of kids once, playing tricks with it outside of their school, and my mates in the canteen told me about them. If you shine one at anybody it sort of dazzles them, blinds them really.'

'So what did you do with it?'

'I— Well, I picked it up, ma'am. Put the cap back on and slipped it into my pocket. I just thought I should. Because of the way it was where it was, sort of pointing to— To the scene.'

'And where is it now? Still in your coat pocket?'

'Yes. Yes, ma'am.'

'Covered in your prints, I suppose?'

'Oh. Oh, I'm sorr— Well, yes, I suppose it may be.'

'It will be, Constable. It will be. But take it to CID at once. Without putting any more of your greasy dabs on it. It's to go to Fingerprints straight away. You've very probably just described a clue to murder.'

Chapter Three

Making her way slowly up to her office, Harriet found herself in a dilemma. She now had little doubt, however minimal the evidence, that a second police officer had been deliberately killed in the area under her charge. If so, the two killings might well be connected. Perhaps they almost certainly were. All right, the presence of a laser pen – electronic blackboard pointer, and dangerous toy – at the scene of Rukshana Syed's death was not conclusive. It could have been there simply by the merest coincidence. But PC Wilkinson, plainly not the most imaginative of men, had nevertheless been struck by the seemingly clear intention of it being put there on the kerb pointing at the dead girl's mangled body.

It did all add up, say what you like, to a possible scenario. Rukshana Syed cycling through the rush-hour traffic on her way back to the flat she shared with her boyfriend . . . And someone, someone with a grudge against her, or possibly with a grudge against police officers in general, standing there with a laser pen, something capable of temporarily blinding, waiting his chance . . . And then – luck or clever judgement – when Rukshana was just in front of an oncoming lumbering bus, sending that disorienting beam straight into her eyes. And perhaps, still standing at the kerb, with the packed traffic snarling and jutting its way past, stepping forward and by giving the tottering girl on her bike one quick push making it almost certain the apparent accident was fatal.

And, an inescapable additional consideration coming suddenly to the fore in Harriet's mind, there might be a special motive for such a crime. One that hit at her herself. The *Stop the Rot* campaign had aroused plenty of resentment among local criminals. Parcels of excrement coming through the letter-box were evidence enough of that. And hadn't that pushful crime reporter, Tim Patterson, even suggested, before he was chased away from the scene of Titmuss's death, that his murder could be a reaction to the campaign? So, yes, it was not impossible that someone had decided to deliver a warning, a pair of warnings. To say she had been pushing too hard.

No, damn it, she thought, I have not. Fire must be fought with fire. Pay them back in their own coin. Yes.

But – and this was another difficulty – if she rang Froggy Froggott now, would he shoot down this notion in the way he had shot down the potential importance of that strand of cloth from a donkey jacket? Or, for that matter, the possible, if unlikely, supposition that PC Titmuss had been killed by a woman?

What to do? Go over Froggy's head to the Chief Constable? Not really possible. Then somehow stiffen up that one piece of insubstantial evidence? Yes, at least find out if anyone anywhere had a motive for

ending Rukshana Syed's life. And then either acknowledge that the idea of the two deaths being linked was
not on, or bloody well tell Froggy what he ought to be
made to realise.

And, straight away there was the fact that Rukshana
was living with a boy. Two young people in that situation were always liable to have rows. And examples
enough of such rows leading to murder.

So see the boyfriend. Find out where he had been at
the time of Rukshana's death. Then, if that eliminated
him, there was another line. Rukshana was a Muslim.
And she had left home to live with this boy. Parental
opposition there, almost without a doubt. And more
than a few cases in recent years of a Muslim father, or
an uncle, or even of brothers, executing summary
justice on girls who had 'dishonoured' the family.

But the boyfriend first.

She picked up her phone and called Personnel,
warning herself to go canny in what she said.

'Rob, it's DCI Martens. I'm glad to find you still in
your office.'

'Yes, ma'am? I was just— Just looking up one or two
things. Checking, really. Is it about that mac? I'm afraid
I haven't had a chance to return it yet. But I've got it
here as a matter of fact. Would you like me to bring
it over?'

'No, no. It's something else I'm ringing about. I
want a favour.'

'Yes, yes. Whatever . . .'

'It's about WPC Syed—'

'That poor kid. Do you know exactly what happened, ma'am? I've only heard the bare fact that she's

been killed. But it hit me. I mean, it was because of me in a way that she was accepted on the Force. Lot of opposition. But I thought having a Muslim and a woman on the strength would be a great help with public relations, and I had a word. So now— Well, I feel responsible somehow.'

'That's just nonsense. I still don't know all the circumstances of the accident. On the face of it, it was the girl's own fault. Momentary carelessness. But there is some reason to think it may have been something else.'

'Not a moment of carelessness? But . . .'

'Don't let this go one inch further, Rob, but there is just a possibility that the accident was caused by someone blinding her with the beam from a laser pen.'

'A laser pen? But— But that'd be murder.'

'No, it would not. It might have been some irresponsible kid playing about. But I want to investigate a little, in case it was more than that. Check on all the possibilities. Which is why I called you. I'm told Syed shared a flat with a boyfriend. Can you give me his address?'

'Yes, ma'am, no trouble. As you know, premises where any officer lives have to be approved by their chief officer of police. In practice, actually, I was the one who more or less gave her the permission to move in there. My recommendation's almost always accepted by the Chief's office. Tell you the truth, though, I did have a bit of heart-searching when I knew Rukshana proposed to shack up with this young man. Name of Barstow, Phillip Barstow, a window-cleaner, white. But when she told me they'd been friends for three or four years I thought – well, nowadays – there'd be no harm in it.'

'All right. So let me have that address. And where was she living before? With her parents? I'd better have that address, too, if you've still got it. But I'll see the boyfriend first.'

'I wish you would. You see, I've a feeling no one will have actually told him yet about Rukshana.'

'My duty then.'

Not the easiest thing to have to do. Got to be done.

Although it was not much after half-past eight she found Phillip Barstow in bed. Or rather coming from the bed in his cramped little flat. His right foot was in plaster, and she had heard him laboriously thumping his way to the door when she had rung the bell.

So no question of him being down in Queen Street when Rukshana had been momentarily blinded and perhaps pushed under the wheels of that No 14 bus. But the difficult task still ahead.

'Mr Barstow?'

'That's me.'

'I'm bringing you some bad news. Detective Chief Inspector Martens from Queen Street police station.'

'Rookie? It's something to do with Rookie, isn't it? She should've been back an hour ago. More.'

'Yes. It is WPC Syed. I have to tell you she has been killed in a road accident.'

The boy tottered on his plaster-cased leg.

She took hold of him by the arm.

'You'd better sit down.'

Then, when she saw through the open door inside that he had been in bed, she led him back there.

He lay on top of the thin flower-patterned duvet, shivering.

As soon as she had decided he was in a fit state to listen she spoke.

'It's been a shock to you. But there are things you can tell me that I need to know.'

For some reason this galvanized the boy. He heaved himself halfway up and glared at her.

'Bloody police. Can't you leave me alone? I never wanted Rookie to join. But she had this idea it was a good thing to do, and I wasn't going to stand in her way. And now look what's happened. First, I fall off me ladder, and now this. This.'

'Calm down. There's no need for any of that. Rukshana made her decision and at least she had the guts to go through with it.'

'Yes. Oh, yes. And now she's dead. Dead. And it's all your fault. Your bloody police.'

'No, it is not. Now, I have got some questions for you, and I want to hear your answers. Without any more yelling and cursing.'

A deeply mutinous look. But the boy was silent.

'Right. Now, I have to tell you this. There is some possibility – nothing more than a possibility, you understand – that Rukshana's death was not wholly an accident. It is just possible it was caused deliberately. So, now, are you going to help me find the truth of that by answering my questions?'

It took hardly two seconds before there came a sullen 'All right.'

'Good. Now, is there anybody, anybody that you know of, who might for any reason want Rukshana dead? Think before you answer. And don't hesitate to tell me anything, anything at all you come up with.'

On the bed the boy had flopped back on to his yellowish thin bunched-up pillow. She could see the thoughts passing through his mind.

'Yeah, well, I suppose . . .'

'What? What do you suppose? Speak up.'

'Well, her old man. He's a bugger, and that's all about it. Cut her off, he did, when she come to live with me. Old sod. I wouldn't put it past him to want her dead. I mean, I don't think he would of . . . But you got to see he might of.'

'Right.' She kept her gaze locked on him. 'So, is there anyone else? I don't suppose WPC Syed was a saintly little creature all of the time, so is there anybody she might have rubbed up against? Enough to make them, if they were a bit gone in the head, say, want to kill her?'

The boy glanced from side to side as if looking for some way of escape.

'No,' he burst out at last. 'No, damn you, why should there be? Rookie was a sweet kid. She was as sweet a girl as ever's been. Why are you saying things like that about her? Why? Why?'

Face plunged into yellowy pillow. Hands hard clutching it. The sound of deep groaning sobs.

Rukshana, before she had set up home with Phillip Barstow, had lived right across the other side of the city, and it took Harriet a good hour to get to the place. As she drove, her thoughts kept switching this way and that. Was it possible that Rukshana's own father, or her brothers or uncles, could be so zealous in their religion as to condemn her to death? Certainly there were instances of such zeal. But it was hard to come to terms with it. Yet it could be.

Before setting out she had rung Fingerprints and asked about the laser pen PC Wilkinson had found. No prints besides his. Whoever had laid it down on the kerb where Rukshana Syed had met her death had been wearing thick gloves.

But every so often as she made her way through the miles of the city's suburbs she found herself thinking of something altogether different. Some words Phillip Barstow had shouted out at her from his bed as she had opened the flat door to leave. *God, you're a hard damn bitch.*

Why pay any attention to a shouted insult from a young man she had just brought bad news to? Yet the words did rankle.

Am I a hard bitch? Hard, yes. I've got to be. You've got to be as a police officer. If you want to see that the law is obeyed. And, damn it, that's what I'm here to do. My duty. My task in life, put it that way. But a bitch? No. No, I don't act the way I do out of any personal satisfaction. Others may. Hard bastards, who glory in being hard. Get their kicks like that. And, yes, there are women officers I've come across who are the same. Hard bitches.

But, no, I am not one of those. I am not. I'm hard,

yes. Because I've got to be. I should be. But I'm hard in a good cause.

Yet still those words prickled in her mind. *God, you're a hard damn bitch.*

Eventually she found the small semi-detached house where Rukshana had lived before she had gone to her shared flat, its name *The Refuge* on a scrolly metal plaque on the gate just visible by the light of the nearest street lamp. She was wrestling with the ironwork gate's half-jammed latch when the front door of the house abruptly opened. Blinking in the stream of bright light from it, she made out a bulky man in his early sixties standing there. Spreading, tangled, grey-streaked beard, heavy horn-rim spectacles, a round white cap on his head, baggy pyjama-like garments below.

'What you are wanting?' he barked out.

'It is Mr Syed? Mr Hamid Syed?'

'I am Hamid Syed, yes.'

'Detective Chief Inspector Martens,' she said, advancing up the cement path of the house's neat little front garden holding out her warrant card. 'Mr Syed, may I ask if you have heard the news about your daughter, Rukshana?'

'I have no daughter Rukshana.'

Harriet felt for a moment as if, riding a bicycle, she had come up against a solid brick wall she had had no idea was there. But she knew even as she drew breath that what the aged bearded Muslim had been saying was that he had disowned his daughter. Because she had gone to live with the young window-cleaner? Because she had joined the police?

It was grotesque, she thought. This was Britain, not the wildest depths of Afghanistan.

Well, give him one more chance. She could be mistaken.

'Have I been given the wrong address?' she asked. 'You aren't the father of Woman Police Constable Rukshana Syed?'

'Holy Koran is stating,' the implacable old man said, 'men have authority over women because God has made one superior to the other. I had authority over a daughter. She defied me. She is no longer of my blood.'

She let the words, the flat declaration, settle in her mind for a moment.

All right, yes, that is what he believes. And he is acting on his belief. To the full. He believes he has that authority . . .

In fact, it is just as I believe I have the authority to check and stop the law-breakers, the law-ignorers.

But not the time or place to think about that. What I have to search out is whether in the end it is possible he has done more than disown his daughter. Did he, in fact, stand there in Queen Street shortly after six o'clock this evening, waiting? And then did he flash that laser beam into her eyes? The laser beam of unrelenting justice?

She stood there in front of the upright old man and gave him back hard stare for hard stare.

'Mr Syed, I know very well that Rukshana Syed was your daughter, say what you will. And I have to tell you that she was killed earlier this evening in what appeared to be a road traffic accident.'

'I have no daughter,' the old man repeated, glaring into the darkness.

'Mr Syed, there are aspects of your daughter's death that give rise to inquiries. You may be able to assist. So, can we go inside while I ask you some questions?'

'There are no questions to ask. The girl was not my daughter. She was sinful. God has punished her in this world. He will punish her also in the next.'

Harriet absorbed this. The bitter draught, harming or healing.

'Mr Syed, may I see your wife?'

'My wife was dying one and a half years ago.'

True? Or had she, too, been declared not to exist for some reason? No, there was something in the way this harsh old man had spoken of his wife that made it clear enough that she had indeed simply died.

'Do you have any other relatives, Mr Syed?'

'In Pakistan, yes. In this evil land, no.'

Ask him why he chose to stay in *this evil land*? No point. But if he has no relatives here, then, if Rukshana's death was an inflicted punishment, only he can have inflicted it.

'Mr Syed, it is my duty to put to you certain questions.'

The fiercely bearded figure confronted her like a steady pillar of fire. But after a long minute he visibly relented.

Perhaps, the thought came to her, the word *duty* had got home where the word *daughter* had dropped to the ground.

'Ask then. Ask.'

'Very well. Will you tell me where you were yourself at about six o'clock this evening?'

'I was where I am at six o'clock each and every day.'

'And where is that?'

'At the mosque. For night prayer. Where else?'

All right, there was a small mosque barely a quarter of a mile away. She had noticed its lit-up minaret on her way. If Rukshana's father had really been there round about dusk, then he could not possibly have been waiting there all the way down at Queen Street as the home-going cars and buses had jostled for position.

'Mr Syed,' she said bluntly. 'Can you prove that?'

She received by way of reply a glance of such ferocity that for half a moment she thought of simply taking the rigid old man's word for it. But, no.

'I asked whether you can prove you were at your mosque this evening.'

The silence lengthened slowly out.

'Many men saw me,' came the words at last. 'I spoke with many. Do you wish me to swear on Holy Koran?'

She decided it was enough. The truth. If only because, had this intransigent old man been down in Queen Street causing the death of his daughter, he would surely not, directly questioned, have denied it. An implacable belief in your own truth had its up-side as well as, possibly, its down.

So Froggy Froggott had to be told about the laser pen. On the face of it, there was almost no likelihood of there being any other person who would have wanted to kill Phillip Barstow's *sweet a girl as ever's been*. And, however tenuous the evidence, it was likely indeed that the girl had been deliberately killed. That the blinding beam from a laser pen had been directed into her eyes as she rode her bike beside the packed and dangerous traffic of rush-hour Queen Street, that she had been made to fall under the heavy wheels of that No 14 bus. What finally made that plain was that the laser pen, had she been merely victim of some yobbish horseplay, would never have been set down with evident deliberation pointing to the spot where she had been crushed to death.

So, evidence of murder. And a murder, surely, paralleling the stabbing of PC Titmuss. Froggy Froggott had to be told.

Harriet phoned from home. She did not want to risk the least possibility of any of her side of the conversation being casually overheard.

'Mr Froggott?'

'Who the hell's this?'

He damn well ought to know her voice by now. This was going to be every bit as difficult as she had expected.

'It's DCI Martens here, sir. There's something I think you ought to know in connection with the Titmuss inquiry.'

'What? Another little piece of thread that's going to resolve the whole case in two minutes?'

'No, sir.'

A deep breath.

'It's this, sir. The PC who happened to be the first to get to the scene of WPC Syed's death in Queen Street earlier this evening told me about something he'd noticed there that gave me grounds for suspecting her death was not as accidental as it appeared.'

'Oh, yes?'

He could not have conveyed scepticism more completely had he used every expression of doubt in the dictionary.

'Sir, I feel it's my duty to pass this information on to you.'

'Well, pass it on then. And let me get back to putting my hands on the man who killed one of our own.'

'Yes, sir. It's this then. The constable observed, placed on the kerb at the precise scene of the accident, a laser pen. A laser pen he believed had been put there, on the kerb, with deliberate intent. So as to point directly at the victim. Now, sir, you'll have heard, no doubt, what a laser pen can do if it's shone into some-one's eyes. There've been cases where the victim has been hospitalized, though no lasting damage was—'

'Yes, yes. I know all that. No need to give me the bloody lecture.'

'No, sir. But, sir, wouldn't you agree that the pres-ence of a laser pen there, together with WPC Syed falling off a bicycle, which she was accustomed to use every day to make her way back home, is significant?'

A silence. A long silence.

Can he really be accepting the notion? Even if it's coming from a senior woman police officer? Froggy Froggott?

'Miss Martens, that is the bloody stupidest idea I have ever heard in all my years of service.'

*

Some two hours later Harriet had the sour pleasure of hearing Froggy Froggott's opinion of her theory repeated in public, if in a slightly less aggressive way. Just before going to bed she had switched her radio on to one of the local stations, as she generally did, to see if anything had happened in the city that she should know about.

She found that Froggy was being interviewed. But, perhaps because he had very little to say concerning an investigation that seemed to have had nowhere to go from the very start, he suddenly contrived a heavy lurch of emphasis.

'Well, all I can say is that I'm satisfied the attack on one of my constables was the work of some mindless drug-addict. And we'll get him. Never you fear. You'll have heard, I dare say, that in fact another police officer in the Greater Birchester Force died today. Fell off her bike into the path of a bus.'

Crass sod.

'Now, when two police officers die in such a coincidental manner, you'll be bound sooner or later to get some happy idiots from the media start trying to make out there's a sinister link there. Didn't I hear somebody hinting at that on the radio earlier?'

But the idea was, of course, too attractive for the interviewer not to pursue.

'You mean to say, Superintendent, that this has been suggested? Despite what you've just said, are the police working on the theory that there may be a connection between these two events, the stabbing of Police Constable Titmuss and – we have an item coming up about this – the road accident that killed a woman police constable in Queen Street this evening? Is it being suggested the two deaths are somehow the work of one individual?'

'Well, they're not, let me tell you. Frankly, an idea like that couldn't be more rubbish if it was fished out of a municipal waste-truck.'

And with those words ringing in her ears Harriet took herself off to bed.

Chapter Four

What will I think of my theory tomorrow morning, Harriet asked herself. Because it is only a theory. And, on the face of it, an unlikely one. Someone unknown setting out to kill two police officers? Whatever reason could they have?

She resolved to let a night's sleep and the cold light of morning provide an answer. Then, as she had long trained herself to do, she cut out the troubles and complications of the day, forced herself limb by limb to relax and resolutely peered into the darkness of closed eyes looking for the first glimpses of dream shapes.

But, flicking awake just after 6 a.m., she found, as she took a quick review of the day ahead, no change in her belief that Rukshana Syed's death under the wheels of that last night's rush-hour bus was no accident. It must be linked somehow to the equally sudden stabbing to death of her fellow Greater Birchester Police officer, PC Titmuss. No, nothing for it but to attempt once again to persuade Detective Superintendent Froggott, despite that vigorously uttered *purely ridiculous* on Greater Birchester Radio, that her theory was no stupid notion cooked up by an over-imaginative woman.

In spite of her belief that what you did not want to do should be done at once, she delayed making her call until she had reached her office. Earlier than nine o'clock, she rationalized, she might be unlucky in getting hold of Froggy Froggott. She knew well enough, from his days in charge of B Division, that it was his boast that he was always at his desk before 7 a.m. *You have to get up pretty bloody early to catch the worms while they're still wriggling*; it was one of his often repeated reprimands to any of his subordinates. But in fact, she knew, had he been kept up late during any major investigation, he was apt not to appear in the Incident Room much before nine, letting it be assumed he had been hard at work elsewhere.

She was nevertheless surprised when at five minutes past nine, squaring her shoulders and looking down at the scratch-pad on which she had made careful and logical notes, she put through her call. Froggy had not yet come in.

'I'll ring again in half an hour or so,' she told his secretary, and turned firmly to the regular tasks of her day.

But it was only ten minutes later that her phone rang.

'Miss Martens?'

It was Froggy's much-harassed secretary again. And sounding more than simply harassed.

'Yes?'

'Miss Martens, you were calling Detective Superintendent Froggott— Oh. Oh, Miss Martens, he's dead.'

'Dead? What do you mean *dead*? Has he had a heart attack or . . .? Or . . .?'

Possible, a heart attack. Froggy never one not to sink another pint, eat a bag of chips on the hoof. Think of anything macho, Froggy had had a bash at it.

'Oh, Miss Martens, it's worse than that. It's— It's— He's been murdered, Miss Martens.'

Her voice now was an almost incoherent howl.

'Pull yourself together.'

This girl, the most recent in a long succession of young women who had found working for Froggy more than they could cope with – what was her name? Yes, Marjorie – had a noticeably silly side. Plus, long, out-jutting front teeth.

'Yes. Yes, I will. I'm sorry.'

A heavy sniff down the line.

'Right, now tell me just what is supposed to have happened.'

'It— It's like this, Miss Martens. Or that's what Detective Inspector Coleman, who went out to the house, told me on the phone just now. Mr Froggott had left to come in here early – you know he always liked to be at his desk before anyone else – and then, when his wife didn't hear the car start up, she eventually took a look out of the window to see if anything was the matter. And there he was. Beside the car. Just lying there.'

'Did DI Coleman tell you anything more?' Harriet snapped out the question as she heard the sobs of hysteria gathering once again.

A gulp.

'Well, yes. Yes, he did. Mrs Froggott called an ambulance but the paramedics reported him, Mr Froggott, Detective Super—'

'Yes? They reported him dead?'

'Yes. Yes, they did. Dead. And Mr Coleman said they had the sense to leave him just where he was till he got there. And he said— He said—'

'Yes? Yes? What did he say?'

'Oh, Miss Martens, that he'd been stabbed somehow in his mouth. He must have been crouching to look at one of his car tyres. The air had been let out of it, and— And then they must— Oh, Miss Martens, it's worse.'

'Then? Then? What else happened, for God's sake?'

'A tooth. One of Mr Froggott's teeth had been ripped right out—'

A wail of total incomprehension – natural perhaps in a woman with noticeably prominent teeth herself – and the line went dead.

Harriet, slowly replacing her receiver, thought with sudden abrupt clarity of the conversation she had had outside her house the day before with ex-Sunday School pupil Rob Roberts. Of how he had reeled off for her the whole of the verse from – What was it? Yes, the Book of Exodus – *Life for life, eye for eye, tooth for tooth* . . . Tooth for tooth. Could that be why whoever had killed Froggy Froggott had ripped out one of his big yellowed teeth? Surely it must be. Why else would Froggy's killer have stopped after stabbing him to carry out that un-necessary bizarre act? An act that was an uncanny echo of WPC Syed's death by laser pen, *eye for eye*? An act, surely, confirming beyond any doubt that Rukshana Syed had indeed been murdered? Because both killings must be the work of a mentally disturbed Bible-quoter of some wild sort. No other answer.

And worse. Surely worse. Wasn't he, this killer, a

man who had for some reasonless reason been seized by a monstrous grudge against all police officers? Or perhaps only against all Greater Birchester Police officers.

Her phone rang again.

It took her a few seconds to realize what the sound of it was she had been so lost in plummeting thought. Then she picked up the receiver.

'DCI Martens? The Chief Constable on the line for you.'

'Sir Michael? Yes, sir?'

'Miss Martens, you've heard, no doubt, about Mr Froggott?'

'Just now, sir. From his secretary I'd rung to— On another matter, sir.'

'And she had the details? Passed them on?'

'I think so, sir. Most of them at least. He was stabbed, as I understand it, while he was stooping to examine a deflated tyre on his car? And . . .'

'That tooth. You know about that?'

'Yes, sir.'

'An extraordinary thing. Some madman at work. But Mr Froggott's the third of my officers to die, to be killed, within forty-eight hours. Last night there was—What was her name? The girl who went under a bus? Syed. Yes. WPC Syed. It must have been your Traffic Department that looked into her death, yes?'

'Yes, sir. I'm up-to-date with the circumstances there. And—And, sir, even before Mr Froggott was killed I was already almost certain WPC Syed's death was not the result of an accident. A laser pen was found at the scene, sir. The constable who saw it described it as looking as if it had been laid down on the kerb with its cap off pointing directly to the place where she had been crushed to death. I'm certain – even more so now – that she was deliberately blinded with its beam to make her fall off her cycle into the path of the traffic.'

'Then, if you're right, she was murdered. Do you see the same individual as responsible for all three deaths?'

'It's an almost inescapable conclusion, sir. To my mind. But there is another thing.'

'Yes?'

'Syed was killed, I believe, because somebody shone that laser beam directly into her eye, or eyes. And the person who attacked Mr Froggott stayed at the scene long enough to rip out one of his teeth. That was how it was described to me, sir. *Ripped out.*'

'Yes, DI Coleman reported as much to me. He said the tooth appeared to have been tugged out of Froggott's mouth, using an instrument of some sort. A pair of carpenter's pincers. Pliers, something like that.'

'Yes, sir. And I see that as especially significant. Sir, it may be the sheerest coincidence, but you'll remember, perhaps, that passage in the Book of Exodus. *Life for life, eye for eye, tooth for tooth . . .*'

'Are you telling me, Miss Martens, that this killer is working on those lines? A life for a life, that would be PC Titmuss stabbed in a way that's unaccounted for so far. An eye for an eye, well, if you're right about that laser pen it would seem . . . And now a tooth for a tooth. That's plain enough. So have we got some total maniac to deal with?'

'I'm afraid it all pretty well adds up, sir. And you

know the rest of that quotation, *hand for hand, foot for foot, burning for burning, wound for wound, stripe for stripe.'*

'Good God, the Old Testament in all its ancient savagery.'

'And its ruthless righteousness, sir.'

'Yes. Yes, you're right. And you're saying that this— This fanatic is intending to mete out that sort of weird justice against other members of my Force?'

'I've been thinking about it, sir. It's certainly not something we can afford to ignore.'

'No, you're right. And that only confirms me in a decision I reached when I first heard about Mr Froggott. Miss Martens, I am putting you in charge now, not only of the inquiry into Mr Froggott's death and those two others, but of what I see may very well develop into a major hunt to get to this maniac before he kills another police officer. I am relieving you of all other duties, not without some regret let me say. And I am granting you the acting rank of Detective Superintendent as from today.'

Then began the busiest and most demanding time of any in Harriet's career. She went at once to the new-built A Division station looking out over the calm lawns and lakes of Wellington Gardens with at the far end of them the imposing buildings of City Hall and the Main Post Office and, in the distance behind, the spire of the Cathedral. Very different from the turbulent, crime-ridden streets of B Division.

Rapidly she absorbed the earliest reports on Froggy

Froggott's death. He had been stabbed, the pathologist stated, with a weapon, probably an ordinary kitchen knife, causing a wound that would have required no great force to inflict. Almost certainly then, she reflected, the same knife that had killed PC Titmuss.

Next she arranged to hold a briefing in the big Incident Room which Froggy, splashily regardless of economies, had set up to run the investigation into the death of the lad warmly remembered for his supposed gift for *sticking something in a woman, and it wouldn't be cold steel.* From its platform she took a long surveying glance at the relaxed team of detectives, looking back up at her with easy curiosity or evident scepticism, at the ranks of VDUs, the enormous whiteboards lining the walls, the banks of telephones.

Then she went into action.

'Right, sit up, all of you.'

There were astonished looks. A stir of dismay. From one or two of the older men glares verging on rebellion. But no one spoke, and by the time she had given the room a second long survey no one, from the two detective inspectors she knew by sight to the scatter of fresh-faced young aides to CID, was doing anything but sitting bolt-upright.

'All right. Now let me put you in the picture. By this time you all must know that Mr Froggott was killed at dawn this morning outside his house in Boreham. But what you don't know is that another death besides that of PC Titmuss which you've been investigating, the death of WPC Syed, was not the simple rush-hour road accident it first appeared to be. It, almost without a doubt, was murder too.'

Down on the floor quick looks flashed from face to face. The assembled detectives were not merely sitting up now but were leaning anxiously forward.

'This is why,' she went on, 'the Chief has put one officer, myself, in charge of what he sees now as a triple investigation. But that is by no means all.'

There was a deep silence of expectancy broken only when one of the aides sitting just below the platform croaked out a single interrogative 'Ma'am?' before choking back into embarrassed speechlessness.

She ignored the dying-bird sound. The young man would have worse to utter than an involuntary squawk before she had finished.

'I don't know how familiar any of you are with the Bible,' she resumed.

And it was a credit to the way she was now holding her customarily cynical audience that there was in response not even a murmur of laughter.

'Yes, the Bible. And especially a bit from the Book of Exodus, a bit that goes like this: *Life for life, eye for eye, tooth for tooth* . . . And I think I needn't remind any of you here that the person who killed Mr Froggott this morning did more than stab him, in much the way PC Titmuss was stabbed. He stopped at the scene long enough to wrench from Mr Froggott's mouth a tooth. A tooth. And I should tell you that I have reason to suspect, too, that WPC Syed was made to fall off her bike under the wheels of a bus by having the beam from a laser pen directed into her eyes.'

At this stage of a briefing, in the ordinary way, she would have expected questions. Now there were none.

52

Only looks hard set, as if they were drawn up to her by a giant magnet.

'But let me give you the rest of that quotation from the Book of Exodus. It is this. *Hand for hand, foot for foot, burning for burning, wound for wound, stripe for stripe.*'

Down almost at her feet the aide who had croaked out that *Ma'am* was now turning his right hand round and round in front of himself with a look of puzzlement, and a hint even of plain fear. And there did come a question. From Detective Inspector Coleman, back from supervising the scene of Froggy Froggott's murder, ready to add to the briefing whatever he had just learnt.

'Are you saying, ma'am, that one day some poor bloody police officer is going to get flogged to death by this— This maniac?'

'Yes, they will be. If we don't stop him first. But now, unlike the situation yesterday when Titmuss's stabbing seemed motiveless, we do have something to go on. What we've got to look for is someone with a fierce grudge against, perhaps the police in general, more likely Greater Birchester Police in particular. A grudge that has something to do with an eye, *eye for eye*, the loss of an eye perhaps or possibly only serious damage to one. A loss for which, with good reason or with very little reason, they might blame us. So, the first actions I want giving out are for a long hard trawl through all our own records of claims against us for personal damages, together with inquiries to other forces. I don't know whether such information will have been logged into HOLMES, but that's where massive computers are meant to be able to assist. Right, as soon as this is over I want those actions up and running.'

A buzz of comment down on the floor now. She silenced it with a sharp 'Pay attention.'

She turned to the nearest whiteboard and picked up the pen on the shelf below. Then she wrote out in a column, the pen giving a shrill squeak at every down-stroke, the whole of the Exodus quotation.

> *Life for life*
> *Eye for eye*
> *Tooth for tooth*
> *Hand for hand*
> *Foot for foot*
> *Burning for burning*
> *Wound for wound*
> *Stripe for stripe*

'Now look at those words. All of you. Look at them every day till we have caught the man who, almost for certain, is intent on working his way through that list. And make up your minds: we're going to stop him.'

She looked to see what response she was getting. Intent faces, pursed lips.

'All right, it should be obvious to you all that we know one key factor about this maniac. The words I've just written up here. Each of his murders so far has been tied to that quotation. But he doesn't know we're aware of it. And I don't want him to know.'

Another look round the whole big room.

'So no one, no one at all, is to say a word about the Book of Exodus. Is that understood? No going to the press and getting yourself free drinks on the strength of letting them hear a bit of juicy gossip. Not a word. Anywhere. To anyone.'

From the expectant listeners a few barely audible murmurs.

'A life for a life,' she went on when they had quietened again. 'It may be that this madman is someone who once lost a relative, a lover, anyone dear to them in a way that might conceivably be blamed on Greater Birchester Police. So, I want actions made out on those lines. Looking for someone who may have harboured for years past a hatred of the police that at last burst out in the attack on innocent PC Titmuss, not necessarily the worthiest officer in this Force but a man who certainly did not deserve to be stabbed to death.'

'But Mr Froggott's murder,' DI Coleman asked. 'Are you saying that there's someone out there who had some sort of a grudge against Greater Birchester Police over some dentistry mishap?'

'No. No, I don't think we need go looking for anyone who has a hatred for us over their teeth. I think it's likely Mr Froggott was killed because he said on the radio last night – I expect many of you heard him – he believed PC Titmuss had been killed by a druggie and that WPC Syed's death was totally unconnected. The very vigorous way, in fact, that he put down the idea that WPC Syed was deliberately killed must have simply enraged the man who stabbed PC Titmuss. I hazard a guess that perhaps he had had no idea in his warped mind at that time of doing more than taking, as it were, a life for a life and an eye for an eye. But, when he heard that the pointer he had deliberately left at the scene of his second revenge killing, that laser pen, was being totally ignored, I think at that moment he decided to kill Mr Froggott as well.'

It looked as if her argument, even among the Froggott admirers in A Division CID – and she knew his macho approach had brought him a good many of those – had been accepted. The murmur of agreement, unvoiced but plain.

'Now, a different set of actions will be needed here,' she said. 'Because it's plain to me – and I think Mr Coleman will agree – that whoever killed Mr Froggott must have known more than a little about his regular habits. That, for instance, he always left home to get to his desk very early in the morning. They would need to have known where he lived, the make of his car, and that he left it outside in the road. All of that must be looked into. The house-to-house questionnaires will have to include, not only asking if anyone suspicious was seen in the area, but whether anyone has been making specific inquiries about Mr Froggott's routines. Some little piece of information one of the officers on door-to-door gets may give us the lead we must find. The lead that, Mr Coleman, will do more than just save one of us from being somehow flogged to death. If we work full-out for whatever hours it takes, if we use to the utmost all the resources that are being placed at our disposal – and the Chief has indicated to me that I can have almost anything I ask for – then some slender pointer we pick up may well save the lives of five of our fellow officers. And, remember, not a word about *Life for life, eye for eye*. If that gets out and I find someone in this room was responsible, they won't be off the inquiry, they'll be off the Force.'

The briefing over, Harriet stayed in the Incident Room just long enough to see the actions she had requested beginning to be carried out. She had taken over the office that Froggy Froggott himself had had, only getting his Marjorie – still inclined to moan with misery – to remove the all-too male objects that decorated it, the sports trophies from long-ago rugby triumphs, the girlie calendar, the rack of burnt and battered pipes. With the windows open as wide as they would go to dispel the odour of tobacco she at last found it habitable.

But she had hardly been settled in her chair when another call came from the Chief Constable. One which, with a tinge of irony at the thought of how she had just announced he would give her whatever help she might ask for, she did not wholeheartedly welcome.

'Superintendent,' he said, 'I have just been in touch with the University of North Essex, speaking to the Head of their Psychology Department, one Professor Peter Scholl. I dare say you know of him.'

'Yes, sir. I do.'

She did know. Dr Scholl had in recent years established an enormous media reputation as one of the pioneers in the science of criminal profiling. He had had his triumphs. And some less spoken of non-triumphs. In the police, some senior officers tended to try and secure his services every time they were faced with a murder that was at all complex, or with tracking down a persistent rapist. Among the lower ranks he had, however, plenty of detractors. Jumping on the name he happened to share with the well-known brand of pedicure products, they labelled him Dr Smellyfeet.

Harriet tended to side with that opinion. There was, to her way of thinking, something about his various pronouncements a little slick. With a touch, as well, of something a little too airy-fairy, a little too much ignoring the plain facts of scummy criminal behaviour.

Hence the ironic smile she allowed herself at the far end of the telephone.

'Well, I am happy to tell you,' the Chief went on, 'I have secured Dr Scholl's services in our present trouble. I have no doubt that, if ever a serial killer has to be tracked down by psychological means, the man we are looking for is such a person. And Scholl agrees with me. He's promised to be here as early as tomorrow morning.'

Harriet decided to say in reply nothing about the measures she had already put in hand to trace the killer. She trusted them a good deal more than whatever insights Dr Scholl might provide. But she knew, too, that it could take a very long time to unearth from old records someone with a grudge against Great Birchester Police over the loss of an eye, even if the right pieces of paper existed. The seemingly simpler task of discovering how the killer had known so much about Froggy Froggott's home life might also require long painstaking inquiries. So psychology could yet get there first.

'Then I'll be glad to have Dr Scholl on the team,' she said. 'Thank you very much, sir.'

But, secretly in her head, she echoed *Dr Smellyfeet*.

Chapter Five

By the time Dr Scholl was due to arrive next day Harriet had conducted her 10 a.m. briefing and had a press conference safely out of the way. She had feared to hear – had almost expected to – that during the few hours' sleep she had allowed herself after poring over reports late into the night that there had been yet another killing. Of some police officer found dead with one of his hands missing. That at least had not happened.

But the house-to-house inquiries in the immediate area of Froggy Froggott's home in 'leafy' Boreham, slowed as they had been by an order she had got the Chief to issue that officers in uniform were always to work in pairs, had produced not a single person who had owned to knowledge of his habits. Most of the neighbours, it appeared, had thought the big man they occasionally saw was, not a senior police officer, but either the owner of a chain of betting-shops or, worse, some sort of a criminal himself. His wife – mercifully it had been the Chief who had paid the visit of condolence – was a self-effacing woman who never gossiped with her neighbours and had devoted herself to making the house and garden all that a senior policeman should have.

So far only one person living nearby, the widow of a retired professor of geography at the University, seemed even to have been aware that every weekday at about 6 a.m. the Rover parked outside the Froggott home had been started up and had left at high speed in the direction of the city centre. The full post-mortem report on Froggy's body had yet to come in.

The Area Forensic Laboratory had confirmed that the strand of wool found at the scene of PC Titmuss's death was from a work-stained donkey jacket, now no doubt well impregnated with blood. But the thread was in no way different from any out of the thousands of similar garments made in the past twenty years. Even the extra inquiries she had ordered when it had become clear that Rukshana Syed's death was not an accident had yielded little. The driver of the No 14 bus, re-interviewed to see if he could describe any possible witnesses, had been able to produce nothing better than a 'tallish old duck with a blue sort of hat' striding away from the scene. Door-to-door inquiries in the area around had failed so far to produce any others. The trawl through the records had yet to turn up a case of Greater Birchester Police being accused of causing damage to any person's eye.

Froggy's Marjorie had just left the office after bringing in mid-morning coffee – 'Mr Froggott always liked four chocky bikkies, but I only brought you two' – when she put her head round the door again and announced Dr Scholl.

Just rising from her chair in greeting him, Harriet observed he was much younger than she had expected. A professor to her, if it did not indicate a long white beard and pince-nez, did at least imply a certain degree of age and even some dignity. Dr Scholl, however, looked to be no more than thirty, if that. Pink-faced and eager, almost as a bright schoolboy, he was wearing jeans and a loose dark green jerkin, revealing a sweat-shirt with *Harvard University* written across it.

Despite his youthful look, she was quick to note, he was already going a little bald, his dark curly hair not quite concealing the fresh pink skin of his scalp as he leant forward – he was, she judged, something over six foot – insisting on shaking her hand.

'Let me make something clear straight away, Super-intendent,' he said. 'Though I have come at the urgent request of your Chief Constable – and, I must admit, out of a strong interest myself – I cannot promise necessarily to be any assistance at all.'

'I'll be as frank,' Harriet answered. 'I don't neces-sarily expect you'll be any help. Oh, I'm prepared to admit that, if someone was able to give us an exact description of the circumstances of the person we're looking for, age, occupation, likely area lived in, then it would be not a little useful. But I should add that, even if you did come up with details of that sort, you'd have to present me with pretty convincing arguments before I'd accept them.'

'Well,' Dr Scholl-Dr Smellyfeet smiled, 'I don't think it's very likely I'll give you any such precise infor-mation. The best we psychologists can do, you know, is to point to the signals that a killer cannot help giving when he commits his crime. He leaves a pattern. A pattern he's almost certainly totally unaware of. But one that a trained observer can read. And one where, in a case like this when you're obviously up against a deeply twisted personality, the psychologist can at least show you what perhaps straight police logic has missed.'

'All right, let me tell you what straight police logic has made clear to me so far, and then you can tell me where I've gone wrong.'

Again Dr Scholl smiled. Engagingly, Harriet had to admit.

'Well,' he said, 'until I've seen for myself as much as possible of the work of this Mr Man – shall I call him that? – I'm as much in the dark as you are. It's the actual facts at the scene, things like the precise method of murder and, more important, the oddities left there, that are going to tell me about Mr Man.'

'Well, I assume my Chief has said that when Detective Superintendent Froggott was killed the person who killed him wrenched out one of his teeth and left it beside his body. Is that one of your oddities?'

'It's one of them, yes. When Sir Michael told me about that, I thought I might be able to do some good here. I take it it was facts like that which made you conceive your theory – Sir Michael gave you full credit – that you were up against a serial murderer of police officers holding a grudge linked with that quotation from the Book of Exodus. Let me say, I'd call that excellent psychological profiling.'

'And I'd call it just plain good police work. Logical deduction from the available facts.'

So you needn't think, Dr Smellyfeet, that flattery will get you anywhere.

Nevertheless she agreed, before he left, to his

request to see all the reports, and told him there could be no objection to his going – she would provide him with a car and driver – to the three crime scenes, although work at them had ended long before. And, yes, when DI Coleman was available he could ask him about anything more he might have observed outside the Froggott house.

'And one other thing, Dr Scholl. The press, all of the media in fact: you will give no interviews to them. You will answer no questions.'

She thought that for a moment a flicker of disappointment had passed across his shiningly pink features. But his agreement came immediately.

'I absolutely understand. A first-class decision. You can expect my fullest collaboration.'

So you're prompt to say, Smellyfeet. But I wonder how long you'll be able to stick to your promise.

He appeared, however, to keep his word well enough during the week that followed in which the investigation, though unceasing, brought no reward. Afternoon after afternoon the *Evening Star* splashed the story of the man it called Cop Killer over its front page, seizing on every piece of tittle-tattle it could about the deaths of PC Titmuss and Detective Superintendent Froggott, which so far it knew as the only two murders of police officers. Its scrawled bills all over the city asked time and again, with ill-concealed glee, *Cop Killer: Will There Be Another?* while so-called experts it had brought in pontificated away on its inside pages. To no purpose that Harriet could see.

Each morning, too, its more serious daily sister paper soberly repeated Harriet's press conference assurances that the inquiry was making progress. Had either paper asked to speak to Dr Scholl, she wondered, and had Dr Smellyfeet done as she had asked and actually kept his presence quiet and his mouth shut? Sergeant Sumpter, the Force press officer, a tubby, bouncily self-regarding sometime journalist with whom she had already quarrelled over what he had wanted to tell the world about *Operation Stop the Rot*, as he delighted to call it, was itching to announce that the famed Dr Scholl had been brought in. She had told him that if one word got out about Dr Scholl or about any single thing the public did not need to know he would find himself walking Birchester's streets 'wearing a tall hat'.

Some negative advances the investigation had made. The full post-mortem on Froggy Froggott found that the fatal wound had been made while, presumably puffing a little as he crouched beside his Rover to inspect that deflated tyre, his mouth had been partly open. It had been delivered, the direction of the wound indicated, from behind. More significantly it confirmed that the wound had been inflicted with a knife whose blade was twenty centimetres long, just the same length as the one that had been thrust into PC Titmuss's neck as he had smoked his covert cigarette.

She was still at her desk late at night when, working her way through the standard reports, she came across a complaint from the manager of a butcher's shop in Market Place that a cleaver had been stolen from the cutting block behind the counter of his shop.

At once she knew – though she had no logical reason to believe it – that this was the instrument the killer was going to use to hack off the hand of his next victim.

She picked up her phone.

'I want calls to go at once tonight to every patrolling officer,' she snapped out. 'They're to be doubly alert for any approach made to them by a man who might have concealed, under his coat or in any sort of bag, a butcher's cleaver. And they're to watch their hands if anyone approaches them. Watch their hands as if their lives depended on it. As they very likely do.'

She went on to order an active search. 'Into every dark corner. Anybody suspected, anybody at all, is to be tackled. But both patrolling officers are to act together. Always. Ready for an attack on themselves.'

But it may be too late, she thought. It may be too damn late.

Or will we have to wait? To go on and on waiting till this man chooses to strike again? *Hand for hand.*

She had the orders repeated to every police station in the city, and told the control room she would be in her office all night.

She was dozing in her chair, Froggy Froggott's big tilting black leather one, when the shrill sound of the phone at her elbow brought her crashing back to reality.

Daylight, she noted, just. A glance at the clock. 5.37.

'Ma'am, some bad news.'

She almost snapped out, Froggy-style, *I don't want a bulletin, I want action.*

'Yes?'

'It's another officer killed. Or, actually not an officer. A cadet. Name of Chatterton. One of the B Div patrols found him behind the British Legion club in Queen Street. They said—They said—Ma'am, his hand had been cut off.'

'Right. I know the place. It's only a couple of hundred yards from my old nick. I'll be there in ten minutes. Oh, and I suppose you'd better ring Dr Scholl at his hotel. You've got a number for him? Get a car round there to take him to the scene. Right?'

'Yes, ma'am.'

In the yard behind the British Legion club, on the far edge of B Division's territory, glaring white lighting had chased off the pale glimmer of dawn. The big Scenes-of-Crime van was parked in the street opposite, a bright orange cable stretching across from its quietly rumbling generator. Someone was staggering across the road with another tall light.

'I see you got here on time this once,' she greeted Inspector Palfrey, his lateness on the scene of PC Titmuss's death not forgotten.

'I've been ready for something like this, ma'am,' he answered tersely, before adding with something of a pointed look, 'and, by God, I hope it's the last one.'

And let's hope to God, she thought, that this time something has been left at the scene that gives us a lead. Or it won't be the last one. There will be *foot for foot* . . . And then more.

Cadet Chatterton's body lay on its side, half-twisted round the seatless dry bowl of a disused outside toilet in the corner of the yard. A seventeen-year-old boy in police uniform. The right hand appeared to have been hacked from the arm with two or perhaps three blows. The wound had bled copiously and almost the whole of the toilet's dust-grained concrete floor was black-stained. Yet the youngster's face, despite the terrible manner of his death, looked almost uncannily calm.

It was, Harriet thought, for all the world as if he had chosen this unlikely spot to lie down in and take a quiet snooze.

'You know,' she said to Inspector Palfrey standing almost accusingly behind her, 'I believe he must have been drugged. Somehow drugged. Doesn't it look like it?'

'Well, yes. Yes, ma'am, you're right. It sort of does. That expression on his face, it's been puzzling me all along. But him being drugged could be the explanation. Yet how . . .?'

At once Harriet thought she knew. Into her mind came the rape case that had been one of the last of her concerns before leaving B Division and *Stop the Rot*.

'I think I know how, or can make a damn good guess,' she said. 'A Rohypnol tablet, a Roofie, in something the lad was offered to drink. God knows when or how. But you must know the effect Roofies have. Plenty of canteen culture jokes about putting girlfriends into a trance-like state. If this poor lad was fed a Roofie, it'd be easy enough to have led him round here, settled him down in this quiet corner and then perhaps suffocated him before using that cleaver.'

She looked down once again at the crudely hacked-off stump. A defeat. But, by God, it would be the last.

Chapter Six

Harriet decided to wait for the Area Pathologist, whose immediate presence at the murder scene she had insisted on before leaving her office. If he could give her on the spot a good approximate time for the death, it would be that much quicker to find out where young Chatterton had been when a Rohypnol tablet – high time they brought in that Government order to put blue dye in the damn things – had been slipped into his drink. If that was the case . . .

A narrowed-down search. A loophole of light.

Soon one of the Scenes-of-Crime searchers came up, holding between his transparent gloves a bundle of pale fawn-coloured cloth blotched with darker stains.

'Pushed well in behind that pile of empty casks, sir,' he said to Palfrey.

He let the bundle fall out to its full length.

'A raincoat,' Harriet pounced. 'Our man must have had to leave it here because of those bloodstains. Must have left in a hurry, too, if the best he could do by way of hiding it was to stuff it behind there. This may be his first real mistake, provided Forensic can tell us anything definite about it.'

A surge of hope. Put together the three things, the

chance that some passer-by might have seen someone hurrying away from the club's backyard, the possibly narrow field of opportunity to administer a Rohypnol tablet, and what could be learnt from the raincoat, and *hand for hand* could be the last of the murders. Unless, of course, the bloodstained coat turned out to belong to someone else altogether, left in the yard after a fight of some sort, and it so happened as well that it was impossible to fix on the moment Cadet Chatterton had been given a Roofie.

A car drew to a halt in the street outside and Dr Scholl came striding into the yard, dewily fresh-faced as ever even at this hour.

The Area Pathologist, Harriet thought, was the one who would be really welcome. Someone who could produce hard evidence. But in the meanwhile . . .

She led Dr Smellyfeet over at once to the tumble-down toilet.

Let's see what a little real blood does to him.

To her disappointment, he simply stood there minute after minute looking not so much at Cadet Chatterton and his oddly peaceful face as up and down the cobwebby little lean-to where he lay.

'Well?' she said, when with the arrival of the path-ologist, a deputy, a woman Harriet had never met, he at last broke away,

'There's nothing I can tell you here and now,' Dr Smellyfeet answered. 'You'll have seen, of course, that the poor fellow must have been unconscious before that hand was cut off. Drugged, I imagine. But I'd like to incorporate what I've seen in my Profile, which as a matter of fact I was going to bring you today.'

'I'll be glad to see it, when I've time,' she said. 'But at the moment I'm more interested in the possible evidential value of a bloodstained raincoat we've found. Provided it belonged to the killer, of course.'

'Can I see it?' Dr Smellyfeet said eagerly. 'There's often a lot more to be told about a coat than anything forensic scientists find on it. I might be able to deduce a good deal about Mr Man from the way his coat seems to have been worn, if it just hung loosely or was always tightly belted, how many pockets it has, the general style that attracted him in buying it in the first place.'

'It'll have to go to Forensic first, but I suppose you can have it when they've finished, if inquiries at the club haven't turned up some drunken brawl that ended with a coat lying on the ground here and then stuffed away.'

'Thank you, Superintendent,' he said, not without dryness.

Harriet turned to the pathologist and concentrated her full attention on what she was finding.

Back at her office with such facts in her head as the pathologist – typically cautious – had been willing to tell her, Harriet put in a call to CID at Queen Street. Should be someone in by this time, she told herself.

There was. And happily it was Sergeant Grant, the officer with most experience of Rohypnol as used by thuggish young rapists.

'Yes, ma'am,' she replied, with a hint of a sob in her voice, when Harriet jabbed out her news. 'I did know Mickey Chatterton. Poor devil. Poor little devil. In fact,

I had him under my wing, as you might say, most of yesterday.'

'You did? Right then, tell me everything he did up to, let's say, seven o'clock. Unless that close-mouthed bloody pathologist changes her mind about the approximate time of death when she's done her p.m., seven would be the latest time for him to have been given that Rohypnol.'

'Ma'am. Well, I had young Mickey out with me – your order: go about in pairs when in uniform – still on house-to-house round Queen Street for witnesses to WPC Syed's death. No luck, of course. So, when it was about half-past six, I decided the lad had been on the go long enough. I told him we'd head back to the nick, get changed out of uniform, and call it a day.'

'You were with him all the time till you got back to the station? He didn't stay behind somewhere towards the end, offered a cup of tea or something?'

'No, ma'am. He was with me all afternoon and right up until we walked into the nick. I said I'd meet him in the canteen then, soon as I'd been to the loo. But when I got back – I'd taken a few extra minutes to get out of uniform while I was at it – he'd gone. I wasn't particularly worried. Thought a kid like him'd prefer to go off with his mates.'

'So you didn't see him again after – what? – seven thirty?'

'More like seven fifteen, ma'am.'

'You realize he was wearing uniform when he was found?'

'No. No, ma'am, I didn't. The stupid— He shouldn't have. He should not have. I'd distinctly said to him that we'd both have to change. Your order's very clear. No one to be out in the streets in uniform unless accompanied by another officer. And, you know, Mickey wasn't a lad to disobey orders just to be clever. That's what hit me so badly – him being a really good and useful lad – when you told me just now.'

'Well, whatever reason he had, or didn't have, he was in uniform when he was killed. I suppose, in fact, if he'd obeyed orders he'd be alive now. As it is, we'll have to go to every pub, every café, every amusement arcade in the area to see if we get a sighting of him.'

And all the time the *Evening Star*'s famous Cop Killer will be looking for his next victim. Perhaps he's waiting somewhere even now. With that cleaver. Waiting for a chance to cut off some officer's foot and leave him, leave him or her, to bleed to death the way young Chatterton did.

Unless that bloodstained coat in the yard there turns out to have some solid evidential value. Unless, the best hope surely, we do find just where Chatterton had that Roofie put in his drink. Or unless Dr Smelly-feet's Profile comes up with some startling insight. Startling and accurate.

Her phone buzzed.

'Superintendent Martens?'

The Chief Constable. Another of his increasingly anxious, urgent and pointless calls?

'Yes, sir.'

'I've been thinking, Miss Martens. I take it we're all agreed this man is a lunatic – or whatever we're supposed to call them nowadays.'

'There can hardly be any doubt of that, sir.'

'Yes. Well, then, I've been wondering if he might be susceptible to an appeal. He must have— He may have periods of lucidity. And if in one of them he reads, or sees on television, a reasoned appeal to him to give himself up . . . If we say something on the lines of *Come forward now. You plainly need help* . . . We should get that Press Officer, what's his name . . .'

'Sergeant Sumpter, sir.'

'Yes. Yes, he could decide on the exact wording, or whether you should give an interview on those lines yourself, or someone else should.'

Rob Roberts? If you want the human touch . . . The bloody sight too much of the human touch.

'Yes, sir. I'll certainly give it my consideration. Or, perhaps, I could talk to Dr Scholl about it?'

'Good idea. Yes, excellent. Do that.'

Putting down the phone, Harriet realized it was almost time for the daily briefing. And, tired and battered by events as she was, fighting the fatigue of an almost sleepless night in Froggy Froggott's big black chair, how was she going once again to impress her will on the men and women under her command? In face of the bleak, black news she would be updating? More than a few of the officers might have known young Chatterton at least to talk to. His sort of keen youngster would seize every opportunity to question real detectives. How, with the pitifully few forward-pointing facts she had got to give out, could she force into each one of the team the determination within herself?

Some new facts she did have. Reports had been coming in to her from the moment she had got back to her office. Negative reports, however. Young Chatterton

had been seen in the Queen Street canteen at somewhere between quarter past seven and half-past the
evening before. And, so far, from then onwards until his
body had been found at twenty-eight minutes past five
next morning by two patrolling constables, obeying her
own order to look into every dark corner for a cleaver-
wielding maniac, he had not been seen by anyone
anywhere.

So where had he been when someone slipped that
Rohypnol tablet into something he was about to drink,
she asked the circle of intent faces in front of her.

She got only the merest floating suggestions. And
always the thought came dragging back to her that the
individual Dr Smellyfeet insisted on calling Mr Man
had now with this death *hand for hand* clearly launched
into his whole crusade aimed at the officers of Greater
Birchester Police. If originally his object had been to do
no more than take a life for a life and to kill once *eye for
eye*, with the rebuff he had had when Froggy Froggott
had scorned the idea that those two deaths were a joint
revenge he had, it was clear now, embarked on fulfil-
ling the whole uncompromising Exodus injunction.

So now at once *foot for foot* must be in his mind. If in
contriving this it might seem he was setting himself
an unnecessarily perverse and complex task, the same
could have been said of his arranging a murder to put
into reality *hand for hand*. Yet he had done it.

But how? How? Where in the last few hours of his
life had Cadet Chatterton accepted a drink from a
stranger?

Yet the briefing, she thought as at last she left the
room, had in the end gone better than she could have

expected. There had been no need to infuse any extra determination. The killing of yet another one who had 'worn the cloth', even if he had not done so for more than a few months, had been enough to tauten faces as they looked up at her, to bring questions and suggestions that eventually had crackled with frustrated energy.

Now, the thought came dully into her head, in less than half an hour I'm faced with the daily press conference, with accounting to the hungry and querulous media for my failure to stop 'Cop Killer' before another death had been added to the toll. And no point any longer in concealing that WPC Syed's death had been one in that toll. The coincidence would be too much.

There came a brisk knock on her door.

'Come in.'

Dr Smellyfeet.

All I need.

'Well,' he said, exuding a cheerful confidence the more irritating for showing no sign of his having been called out of bed before six, 'here we are at last. The Profile. I'm sorry I've been so long over it really, but it wasn't until late last night I got enough in my computer back at the uni to produce a properly robust theory.'

He tapped with long pink fingers at an enormously thick blue cardboard file held precariously under his left arm.

'Look,' Harriet said. 'I've got a press conference in twenty minutes. This will really have to wait.'

'Well, it could. Of course, it could. But I rather think you'll be a good deal better armed for what they may throw at you at that conference if you listen to some of the things I can tell you. My whole theory is here, of course, the lot, maps, graphs, tables. But I could give you a quick run-down of the key points.'

Patience. At least for a quarter of an hour. No, ten minutes.

'All right. Take a seat. And shoot.'

'Yes. Now, the first thing is I've established the area in which, in all probability, Mr Man lives.'

'Well, where?'

'Very simple. All four crimes, with the account-able exception of Detective Superintendent Froggott's death, occurred within a circle with a radius of less than half a mile. A circle which actually has its centre more or less where your Queen Street police station comes. Or, to be strictly accurate, it's a sort of flattened circle. Because across the northern edge of it there runs the Birchester–Liverpool Canal. Look at this sketch map I've made.'

He planked the fat file on her desk, scrabbled in it for a moment and produced a thick sheet of paper.

'Look, here's the circle with Queen Street police station at the centre. But there, along the top of it, there's a straight line cutting off the upper segment. That's the canal. So the area I've picked out is a sort of cup shape. Okay?'

'Yes, I can just about follow that. I'm not exactly a simpleton, you know.'

'No, no. I'm sorry. But I am right, aren't I, in thinking that the communities on either side of the canal are distinctly different?'

Harriet thought for a moment.

'I don't know about that. It's a straightforward

working-class area on either bank. Or, rather, that's what it used to be. A lot of it is sheer slum nowadays. But I can't see the areas either side of the canal are particularly different.'

'Can't you? Do you know anything about football?'

'Football?'

'Yes. I assume you know there are two Premiership teams based in Birchester, and—'

'Of course, I know that. For God's sake, I am a Birchester police officer.'

'Well then, do you know who people on the north side of the canal support?'

Less than a moment's thought. Vivid memories of hundreds of green-and-white coloured scarves.

'Yes. They're United supporters.'

'Right. And on the south—'

'You're right, of course. Rovers fans. So, yes, I suppose you're correct. The people on each side of the canal are to some extent different.'

'Which is why I had no hesitation in drawing that more or less straight line – curves a bit, actually – across the top of the circle. Very well, on the basis of previous successful experiences with serial killer cases, we can now say the probabilities are that Mr Man lives inside my flat-topped circle, or somewhere not too far from it, on the south side of the Birchester–Liverpool Canal.'

'So all we've got to do now is visit – what? – ten thousand homes?'

'Oh, I can give you more help than that. I can tell you the sort of person you should be looking for in those homes.'

She fought off the yellowy cloud of her depression.

'All right. I'm listening.'

'Well, to begin with, you should expect to find a man who is at the higher end of the manual worker class. We know from the evidence of the fibre from that donkey jacket that Mr Man is an industrial worker of some sort, and from—'

'We know nothing of the kind,' she snapped out in irritation. 'All we've got as good evidence is a thread, almost certainly from a donkey jacket, yes, found caught on the wall of the passageway where PC Titmuss was stabbed. Even if it did come from the killer's coat, we don't know that the coat actually belongs to him. It may have been borrowed. Or even bought secondhand to use to hide in at the end of that passageway.'

'Yes, there is that. I grant you that. But, always provided the thread did come from the murderer's donkey jacket, then I think you'll agree it indicates he has a manual worker background. And, I may add, the fawn-coloured raincoat you told me about this morning, turned out to be, if not quite what you'd expect a hefty mechanic to wear – it's rather small in fact – a mass-produced garment such as a person at that point in the social scale might possess.'

Or a senior woman police officer who liked not too feminine outerwear and was not desperate about appearing designer-dressed . . .

But she held her tongue.

'Now, I mentioned that Mr Man almost certainly comes from the upper end of the manual worker class. Why? Because he's a planner. All the evidence goes to show he's an individual who's habitually used to working out carefully his next move. And that won't apply simply to his moves as a killer. No, the cast of mind is there. And will appear in everything he does. Hence he'll have risen up to become a foreman, that sort of status at least. Until something became too much for him and he was sectioned.'

'Sectioned? How do you know he's been mentally ill? If you've got a name—'

Now Dr Smellyfeet did lose his cool.

'Superintendent, if I'd had even a short list of names, they'd have been on your desk within two minutes of my getting them.'

'Yes. Yes, sorry. I realize that. All you were saying – was it? – was that it's likely, or very likely, this man has been in a mental hospital?'

'Yes. Yes, I'm pretty sure that must have been the case. There's every sign in these crimes of mental instability. Even the papers have seen that. They refer to him as a maniac, as often as not.'

'All right. And, of course, we've been working on those lines, certainly ever since WPC Syed's murder. But, let me tell you, we've checked on our computers every name we have who's ever been reported as mentally unstable. And not one of those men checked can be your Mr Man. Yes, there were five or six in and around Birchester who might have been him – not that they had any anti-police record in particular – but each of them had an alibi, double-checked, for at least one of the murders, if not more.'

'Nevertheless I think it probable, at the very least, that Mr Man was kept in confinement for a long period up until recently. That is why the murders did not start until just recently. All that your searches of your computer records prove is that Mr Man has never come under police notice.'

She was going to leave it at that. To heave herself out of her chair and get down to the press conference in good time. But then she remembered there was something she had undertaken to consult Dr Smellyfeet over.

'Oh, there is one thing you could perhaps shed some light on. The Chief's been wondering whether it would do any good to issue an appeal to your Mr Man, beg him to give himself up. Tell him he needs help, that sort of thing.'

'An appeal?'

He thought for a moment.

'No. No, I can't see it. He's a planner, as I said. He thinks ahead. He knows what he intends to do, and I very much doubt if any appeal would make him change his mind.'

'Right. Well, I asked.'

'No, I still believe the picture's something like this: Mr Man was prevented by some circumstance or other from taking his revenge for the ill he believes Greater Birchester Police have done him up until, let's say, a month before the attack on PC Titmuss. If he is obsessed by hatred centred on your Force, for good reason or bad, then it is psychologically impossible that he would go for years and not take action. It's his pattern. He can't escape it. Take it from me.'

'I'll have to. You're the expert we've called in. But actually I can add something that bears out your—' She checked herself from saying *guess*. 'Your theory. We've also been carrying out a search of Greater Birchester Police records and even of the HOLMES computer for anyone who's made a complaint about being mishandled by the Force in a case involving an eye or the eyes. All our more recent records have revealed nothing. The search is still going on. It's a long and painstaking process. We may find something in the end. But it certainly indicates that there was a long gap in time between that injury, if there ever was one, and the first attack or the second *eye for eye* affair.'

'Thank you. I'm glad you realize how useful psychological profiling can be. There are still plenty of muttonheads who think we're as crazy as the people we're called in to evaluate.'

A fellow who's yet to learn that flattery doesn't always wash.

'Make no mistake, I'd much rather be dealing with plain facts.'

'Well, at least let me add one or two other pointers you should find useful. For instance, there's no sexual element involved. I know most laymen think we do nothing but invent fine old sexual fantasies to justify our business. But here's a plain fact for you.'

'I'm glad to hear it.'

'Let me put it this way. Cadet Chatterton's uniform trousers were still zipped up.'

She thought for a moment.

'Point taken.'

And then the glimmer of a thought entered her head.

'Tell me,' she said, 'what did you make of the attitude

81

Chatterton was lying in? That sort of thing is grist to your mill, isn't it?'

'The attitude? Oh, you mean his air of calmness. Well, I see that as being rather more grist to your mill, Superintendent. One of your plain facts pointing to the lad having been drugged. Probably, as you suggested, with Rohypnol.'

'You don't think it's significant that he had to be given a Roofie?'

'I'm not sure what you're driving at.'

'That it wasn't possible for your Mr Man to get hold of the lad by force.'

'I don't quite—'

'Dr Scholl, isn't it just possible that your Mr Man is Mr Woman? Think.'

Chapter Seven

After the press conference, at which Harriet had felt free to announce that Greater Birchester Police was using the famous Dr Peter Scholl to help with the hunt for the killer – she had not dared even hint at the possibility this was not a man but a woman – it took her most of the rest of the day to work her way through his massive Profile. She would read a page, realize the jargon had temporarily deceived her into thinking she had understood, go back and laboriously work out the obfuscated meaning.

She had, too, to break off each time that a new report came in. Only to feel a new jab of disappointment when it was not of a sighting of Cadet Chatterton in any of the possible pubs or cafés where he might have drunk a beer or a cup of tea, or in the arcades where he might, like any other teenager, have been playing the machines. Eventually, late in the evening, she had to admit the inquiries were now unlikely to produce a result. Wherever the lad had gone after leaving Queen Street police station no one had particularly noticed him, strange as it seemed. So in all probability they would find no witness to him taking some drink into which his killer had slipped a daze-inducing Rohypnol tablet, get no description of the person who had been with him. The end of a once hopeful trail. Just as the less hopeful hunt for witnesses to WPC Syed's death and for people in the suburb of Boreham who had been questioned by some stranger about Froggy Froggott's habits had equally petered out into nothingness.

She had had to abandon her wrestling with Dr Smellyfeet's academic prose, too, when the Chief Constable rang to know what his tame expert's reaction had been to his idea of issuing an appeal hoping to catch the killer in a lucid period. He had needed firm handling to be convinced that the idea had definitely been turned down.

'Well, I suppose the man knows his business . . !'

'Yes, sir. I'm just reading the Profile he's handed in. It shows every sign of his competence.'

'And light? Does it throw light on who we're looking for?'

'Yes, sir. It does. A little. But I rather think it will be more useful to us after we've laid hands on—' She checked just for an instant. 'After we've laid hands on *him*, sir.'

'And are you going to do that, Miss Martens? Are you going to lay hands on this madman before he lays his hands on yet another of my officers?'

Back at home, almost too weary to make herself a meal, she found she could not stop herself thinking about Dr Smellyfeet's reaction to her proposal that they could be looking not for *Mr Man* but for a woman.

'No,' he had said. 'No, Superintendent, you're simply talking nonsense.'

'Or is it just that I'm contradicting the whole basis of this great thick Profile?'

'No, it's not.'

Dr Smellyfeet had had the grace then to look a little ashamed at the heat he had shown.

'Well,' he had said, 'it's not that altogether that riles me. I hope I can take criticism, even somewhat unjust criticism. But I really don't think that's why I believe you're talking non— Why I feel you're quite wrong. No, I'm basing my objection strictly on the psychological facts in the Profile.'

'All right, but just consider some other facts, of a different sort. Number One, why did our killer have to drug a lad like Chatterton before attempting to cut off his hand? Answer, in my book, because she – she – is too physically weak to do anything else. Number Two: that raincoat left behind in the British Legion yard, a raincoat not unlike one I had myself until a couple of years ago. A raincoat which you said was *not quite what you'd expect a hefty mechanic to wear.* Just how big or small was it, Doctor? Tell me.'

Dr Smellyfeet had bitten his lower lip at that.

'It was smaller perhaps than I indicated.'

'Right. A woman's coat. And something else you pointed out to me: that young Chatterton's fly was still done up. That not *indicate* anything to you?'

'Well, of course you'll find nothing in the Profile that absolutely contradicts your view that Mr— That the person we're looking for is a woman. But all the same . . . Of course, there have been instances of female serial killers, but really they're few and far between. No, Superintendent, you've made me think, but in the end I don't accept your proposition.'

'Let's say not a proposition, just a suggestion.'

'All right. Then I don't think there's really any merit in your suggestion. Or not until we learn something that seems to endorse it.'

'Such as the fact that, if this person is motivated by deep-seated resentment at some injury received at the hands of the Greater Birchester Police, then it's perhaps more likely it was a physically weak person rather than a physically strong one who received that injury?'

'Yes. There may be something in that. But you can't rule out a man, *my Mr Man*, as you constantly call him, having been injured by a member of your Force. Injured in the eye, probably. And feeling deep resentment afterwards.'

'No, as I said, a suggestion only. But, taking it into account, do you still think there'd be no point in appealing to – shall we say *to the person*? – to come forward and get help?'

Once more Dr Scholl had considered.

'No,' he had said after a little. 'No, either man or woman, I don't see anyone as obsessed as they are responding to any sort of appeal.'

'Not even . . .' She had been thinking as she spoke. 'Not even to a direct challenge? Might not something like that bring whoever it is out into the open?'

More thought. Much more.

'I suppose it might. Yes, it might. But surely that's not on the cards, is it? You're thinking of a challenge from you as heading the hunt to— To him or her? To do what? To meet you face to face at some place where you'd both be on equal terms? Come on, of course Sir Michael would never agree to any such— Well, I should have to call it a stunt.'

'Yes. In so far as I'd thought at all, that must have been what I had in mind, a stunt, if you like. One that, if it was successful, would cease to be a stunt and become – what? – a dangerous but justifiable stroke. But you're correct. The Chief would never allow it. And quite right, too, really.'

Over and over that conversation she went until eventually she made herself go to bed, and at last rigorously apply her sleep-inducing technique.

No change when she got to her desk next day. No night attack on any patrolling pair of officers. No hulking Mr Man coming at them sweeping his stolen cleaver towards their feet. Not even any suspicious individuals, of either sex, found lurking anywhere. The only new factor worth anything was the full report from Forensic on the raincoat from the British Legion yard. She felt a flicker of irony as she read the words *a buttonless unisex garment*, but there was nothing to point to its possible ownership. The blood was the same group as Cadet Chatterton's. A DNA match would take longer to obtain. Two more sections of the trawl through police records for compensation claims that had been rejected. And nothing found.

The 10 a.m. briefing with little to enthuse it. An 11 a.m press conference, with enough questions about Dr Scholl to cover up the fact that she had almost nothing to say. And a mercifully silent, for once, Tim Patterson, crime reporter.

Then, just after midday, toothy Marjorie burst in thrusting out in front of herself like some sort of every-which-way kitchen apron the first edition of the *Evening Star*.

'What—'

'Miss Martens. I think— Miss Martens, you ought to see this.'

She managed to batter the paper down, more or less flat, on the desk. And the words of its thick black front-page headline were plain to see.

AN EYE FOR AN EYE

She read the heavy print text below at lightning speed. And it was plain, despite the slight misquotation of the big headline, that *Tim Patterson, Evening Star Crime Reporter* had acquired full details of the link between the Book of Exodus and the paper's favourite headline Cop Killer. In a separate squared-off panel the whole of the passage was quoted, word for biblical word.

Life for life
Eye for eye
Tooth for tooth
Hand for hand
Foot for foot
Burning for burning
Wound for wound
Stripe for stripe
(Canon Walter Smith writes, page 6)

The full theological position. That should grab *Evening Star* readers all right.

The phone buzzed.

'Yes?'

'The Chief Constable for you, Superintendent.'

'Good morning, sir.'

'You've seen the early *Evening Star*, Superintendent?'

'Yes, sir.'

'I understood we were keeping the connection with the Book of Exodus strictly secret. I thought it was your view, as it was mine, that it was important the killer should not realize we knew of that foul agenda of his.'

'Yes, sir. That was my view. And it still is.'

'Then you didn't authorize the story in this rag?'

'No, sir.'

'So what happened, Miss Martens? This is a serious breach of discipline.'

'It is, sir. And when I've got this killer safely locked away, I will investigate.'

'Yes. Yes, well, I'm glad to find you've got your priorities right, Superintendent.'

But who might it be all the same, the thought could not be kept out of her head. How many people had known about that list? Everyone at the daily briefings: they had had to know. So, despite all warnings, could it be one of them? Tim Patterson, notoriously, was free with drinks and flattery. Someone could have . . . But it seemed unlikely. For one thing they were all working night and day on the hunt. For another, they were dedicated if ever detectives were. The deaths of three colleagues, four now, had to be avenged. So no merry evenings with young Patterson.

Right, leave it. *When I've got this killer safely locked away, I will investigate.*

More to the point, what is seeing these words blazoned across the front page of the *Evening Star* going to do to the creature methodically working through that primitive list? And, if he – or she – is living in the city, within Dr Smellyfeet's famous flat-topped circle centred on Queen Street, almost for a certainty they will see the *Evening Star*. And have probably been lapping up, too, the taunts printed in its pages about police failures.

Harriet picked up her phone, got through to the office allocated to Dr Scholl and urgently summoned him.

'The *Evening Star*, Doctor?' she shot out as he entered. 'You've seen it?'

'Yes. And it's not what I'd have wanted to see.'

'You think it's bad for us, then? I was afraid of that.'

'Yes. If ever anything was wanted to feed this killer's obsession it will be seeing those words set out where everyone can read them.'

A verdict from Dr Smellyfeet she could not quarrel with.

She sat for a second or two staring down at the words from Exodus in their set-aside panel on the billowing, dismembered *Evening Star*.

'One thing,' she said eventually. 'This removes any temptation I may have had to issue some sort of personal challenge.'

'Yes, I hardly think we need anything more just now to stir him up.'

'Or her.'

More of a jibe, in anger at what had happened, than any reinforced belief that Mr Man was a woman.

'I'm sorry,' she added quickly. 'Shouldn't have said that. Only confuses the issue. And that is, quite simply, what will seeing this list' – she gave a quick stab at the spread-about paper – 'make the killer do?'

Dr Scholl did not need time for reflection.

'I'd stake my reputation,' he said, 'on the plan for the next one, for *foot for foot*, being already well worked out. It may be, though, that this will make him act more quickly than he had intended. And, if so – a big *if*, mind – then it may give you a better opportunity to catch him, if he takes more risks than he's planned. But, on the other hand, his plan might as yet have been only in embryo. And then, though he may speed things up a little, he almost certainly will make all the more certain of every step he's going to take.'

'So it's wait and see which way the cat jumps? That's all?'

'I'm afraid I can't do better than that. We're not magicians, us psychologists, you know. However much some sections of the media like to portray us as such.'

'No, I don't think you're magicians. And I rather suspect that, in saying what you have, you've already gone further out on a limb than you should have done. I don't see, really, what else you could have told me that would help. All I can do is repeat everything I've told the team so far, issue yet another warning to every patrolling officer – to every officer in uniform – to be on their guard against a maniac wielding that same butcher's cleaver that hacked off poor young Chatterton's hand, and— And hope!'

It began to seem, as the afternoon stretched into evening, that the killer knowing the police had had the Exodus quotation in front of them all the while was not going to rush into action. No report of anything suspicious came in from the redoubled patrols, all of them now in possession of the ominous words *foot for foot*.

The early evening local television news made almost as much play with Exodus as Tim Patterson had done in the midday edition of the *Evening Star*. So there could hardly be any doubt that the killer must be aware that the police had all along been alert to the Book of Exodus. Even if the killer was illiterate – and Dr Smellyfeet's profile had argued well for a fair degree of intelligence – they could not now but know that the police they hated were ready for their next move. *Foot for foot.*

In the end Harriet went home earlier than she had done on any night since she had found herself in charge of the hunt. She had done everything she could think of. The only thing now seemed to be to wait for the killer to attempt to murder some Greater Birchester Police officer somewhere, almost certainly by hacking off a foot as he had hacked off Cadet Chatterton's hand, and to trust that the warnings she had issued would frustrate him.

Rage had boiled up in her at the impotence forced

upon her. Action. She wanted action. Thoughts of the days, not at all long ago, when she had been running *Stop the Rot* came enviously back to her. She had been active then at every moment, taking the battle to the enemy, taking every least little skirmish to the wrong-doers, at the sharp end herself often as not, stopping every least infringement of the law.

At home in her early bed she had needed all the willpower she possessed to make herself relax, peer with closed eyes for such harbingers of sleep as her subconscious might send flicking up from the depths, odd, unaccountable, ridiculous, but presaging useful oblivion.

Though in the end she had dragooned herself into six hours of restorative sleep, next day they seemed hardly worth having had. There were no demands on her that she could not have responded to had she gone without rest for forty-eight hours.

At 10 a.m. she had taken the briefing. But she had not been able to bring to her team any new development that might give them a fresh impetus. There had been no developments to bring. In the final minutes she referred shortly to the leaking of the Exodus quote, taking as she did so a covert look round at the faces in front of her. But, so far as she could tell, there was not a glimmer, not a tightening of the lips, not a quick glance down, that indicated guilt.

She left it.

Each morning at ten in the days that followed she took her briefing. Every day at eleven or twelve she met the media. A camera from the local TV was always there, waiting with its little red eye to pounce if there was any sort of sensation. The national press had ceased to take much interest when each day there was nothing new to say. But the *Evening Star* sent Tim Patterson faithfully morning after morning and always he had his maliciously delivered questions designed to find some new stick with which to beat Greater Birchester Police.

Six days a week, too, the paper printed the death-dealing litany. For three days the panel had appeared on the front page, though such theological comments – adroitly taking the sting out of the uncompromising Old Testament words – that Canon Walter Smith, writer of the paper's Saturday Sermon, had made on its first appearance were not repeated. After that the panel was relegated to Page Two. But always in the same accusing shape.

And each day Harriet made herself look at it.

Ten days after its first appearance it was sharing Page Two with a few other items of Birchester crime, many of which, Harriet thought, would not have come into existence if she had been there to keep *Stop the Rot* going as unremittingly as it should.

Then, on the eleventh day, a comparatively small headline there caught her eye.

Chapter Eight

All the small headline had said was *Fatal Step*. But, full as Harriet's mind was with the thought of the fatality she expected, she attacked the three short paragraphs below as if each line might hide a secret she had to discover. The fatal step, she found however, had not been taken by a police officer. The paragraphs simply told of the seemingly accidental death of one George Studley, a gamekeeper, from a village called West-holme, some fifteen miles from central Birchester. Out at night patrolling the woods, his foot had caught in a snare and the shotgun he had let fall appeared to have accidentally discharged, wounding him in the head. He had not been able, apparently, to free himself and had been too far from the nearest houses for his shouts to be heard. Only when his wife found he had not come home from his night patrol was he discovered, dead from his injuries.

It was surprising, Harriet thought, that the item had been allowed to appear on the same page as the paper's continuing campaign centred on their Cop Killer's *foot for foot* threat. But no doubt somebody at the paper had made the connection and had then made sure there was no reference to it in the story. The dead man's family would be justifiably distressed at any claim the death was other than accidental.

Yet . . .

Harriet decided, however much the *Evening Star* had disallowed the *foot for foot* coincidence, it was something she could not let pass altogether. A call to the outlying Greater Birchester Police station covering Westholme would set her mind at rest.

Yes, Inspector Young said, the report in the *Evening Star* had got the facts right.

'For once . . .' she murmured.

The sergeant who had investigated had been satisfied – a post-mortem had yet to be held – that it was an accident, though he had thought loss of blood from the deep cut the snare had made rather than from the shotgun wound had been the actual cause of death. He had been surprised, however, that George Studley, a steady, careful man, had let himself be caught in a snare. He had known him well 'back in his days in uniform when he had the police house at West-holme—'

'What? What's that you're saying? This— This George Studley was a former village constable?'

'Yes. Yes, ma'am. He was out at Westholme right up until the reorganization when we began policing the village from here. Studley resigned then, bought the police house for himself, and found a job as game-keeper for Colonel Timperley, the local landowner.'

'Inspector, I'm coming out to you. Make sure the sergeant who went to the scene of Studley's death is there to meet me.'

A police officer, or at least a former policeman,

killed when he was caught by his foot in a snare. *Foot for foot*. Exodus, xxi, 23.

George Studley's widow, when Sergeant Franks introduced Harriet to her, proved to be a solid woman of sixty or so, stunned into almost complete silence by her husband's death. She sat on a flowered-print sofa in what must once have been the office in the former police house, knees apart, big weather-reddened face inexpressive, body immovable as a haystack.

Harriet offered her condolences. When her few words evoked no response she went in bluntly with the question that should give her the answer, yes or no, to the possibility that had brought her all the way out to Westholme.

'Mrs Studley, tell me, were you surprised that your husband caught his foot in that snare?'

The newly made widow was not put out by this direct approach.

'I was,' she said, woodenly. 'Still am. Not like my George, that weren't. Why I'm pleased police are taking proper notice now.'

She turned her head to give Sergeant Franks a long steady stare.

Harriet took in the full implications.

So it was *Yes*. Or certainly not *No*. Move on then, move on.

'Your husband had been a gamekeeper for Colonel Timperley for a good many years? He knew the woods well. Is that it?'

'Aye.'

'Are many snares set in the woods, do you know?'

'Nay, I suppose a poacher might set one. But my George never said owt. Or not till Cousin Grace kept asking, when she came here.'

A different bell suddenly beginning to ring, if still far off.

'She paid you a visit, your cousin? Does she come often?'

Mrs Studley grunted out a laugh.

'Come? She's not been here for years.'

The bell ringing a little more loudly.

'When was it that she came then?'

'Last month. Must've been.'

'Last month? Was that by invitation?'

'Nay. I'd never invite her, cousin though she be. Not the way she is. And my George never did care for her. Too much of the *I'm right* about her for him.'

Harriet dismissed that.

'But you weren't pleased either?' she said. 'Why was that?'

'Who'd be pleased to have a loony come knocking at their door? Looking like she'd been living in a dustbin. An' smelling like it, too. No coat to her back. A dress you couldn't tell whether it were green or brown, hanging down from her like a great long strip o' carpet. A great big blue woolly hat on top o' her head.'

A blue woolly hat. Something more clicked in Harriet's mind. The description the bus driver whose vehicle had crushed WPC Syed had eventually given of the only witness he had noticed. She was, he had said, *a tallish old duck with a blue sort of hat*. So if after all the person they were hunting was, as she had postulated, a woman, could she be this woman who had come unexpectedly visiting here? Only shortly before the former Greater Birchester Police constable who lived in the house had been found dead with his foot deeply cut by the wire of a snare?

Yes. It was her. It must be. The *Evening Star*'s Cop Killer, Dr Smellyfeet's *Mr Man*, Mrs Studley's Cousin Grace.

'Oh, aye,' Mrs Studley was ploughing on, a straight furrow. 'Looking like a loony. And being one. Grace were that, all right. She were in the bin for years. And I don't know as how any of 'em gets cured proper, for all they say.'

'And she suddenly turned up here? Do you remember just when?'

'End of last month. Be last Sunday in March.'

Bell ringing steadily now. Saying something that had been altogether unexpected. If just guessed at earlier.

'Right. Your Cousin Grace— What's her full name, by the way?'

'Grace Brown. Grace Yelland, as was. Same as me, though we're far enough apart as family. Married Jack Brown at seventeen she did. A' course he's left her.'

'Oh. Why was that?'

'She couldn't be lived with, that's why. Not after losing the baby.'

'She lost a baby?'

Life for life. This must beyond doubt be . . .

'Aye, she did that. An' it were her last chance, so I heard tell. They'd wanted and wanted, but none came. Not till this 'un, when she were almost too old for it.'

'Tell me, do you know how she came to lose the baby? Was it because of some accident?'

The question she hardly dared to put.

'Aye. You're right there. An accident it were. The way of it was this, as I heard. She were always overgone in religion, you know, the way some are. The one time I visited there, it were prayers before, prayers after, and as many in between as she could put in. Her Jack weren't so keen on 'em, but she never stopped. And it were when she were out protesting over summat to do wi' religion that she got hit and lost the little 'un.'

Bells almost blotting out all thought. The answer. The absolute answer.

'Do you know more details of that?'

'Well, I don't know about details. I'm sure we never heard all the rights and wrongs of it. I don't rightly know if I even should say anything, seeing as how you're the police.'

'Police? It was something to do with the police? But you can tell me. I'm more than used to hearing the police abused.'

'Aye. Well, this is what we heard. Mind you, it were a long while since. She never said no more about it when she come last month.'

'No, but never mind. Just tell me what it was that you did hear.'

Mrs Studley, sitting with huge solidity on the flower-print sofa, seemed as unfazed by repeated questions as she would have been outdoors by a passing shower of rain.

'It were one o' your police that hit her, that's what I heard.'

'Hit her? How? You said it was when she was protesting over something? Do you know what it was?'

'Babies, of course. She was one of 'em as believe you should never stop babies coming, an' there were a lot of 'em there o' the same opinion. Well, more than opinion, more like *We be right, and you be wrong.* There they were, so we heard, outside one of they abortion places. An' kicking up a right rampage. Stone throwing, an' all. I don't know what.'

'Yes? And your cousin was there, you say. And in the course of the protest she was hit? Hit by a police officer?'

'Oh, she was that all right. That was when she got blinded in her eye, that was.'

There. It must be it. The killer identified at last. Not Mr Man but Mrs Woman. Mrs Grace Brown.

Now, more to ask.

'And your cousin losing her baby? That was a result of her injury?'

'So she said. So she always said and swore it. Before they took her away. Any time I saw her – an' in them days I saw more on her than I've seen these past five or six year – she were going on about how she'd suffered so an' was getting not a penny compensation. In a rare taking every time we met, she was. A rare taking.'

'And then she was admitted to a mental hospital?'

'Into the loony bin she went, aye.'

'And then, after a good many years— How many years ago was it that this happened? Can you tell me?'

The silence of careful thought.

'Well, it must have been more than six year when we got to know. Aye, six and a whit more. It were while

my George were still police constable. I remember him
telling an' telling me the like of it would never have
happened wi' him.'

'And how long before you got to hear about it had it
happened? Do you remember?'

'Nay, you can't never ask a body to remember that
far back an' get it right.'

'But what would you say? Vaguely?'

'Well, it must have been a good year before we got
to know. A good year. I do recall we were surprised to
know it had happened, an' we not so much as hearing a
word.'

'So could we say eight years in all? About eight
years ago?'

'Aye. I suppose.'

'And then she suddenly turned up here? Where had
she come from? Was it her old home?'

'No. No, it couldn't have been that. Jack sold when
she were put in the bin. Before he went off to Australia.
To forget all about it, poor chap. To forget, if he could,
all about her. And to forget about us, too. We never
heard one word from him after.'

'So you haven't any address for him? But what about
her? She didn't by any chance say where she's living
now?'

'Nay. Not a word did we get about herself. And I
were glad. I'd heard all too much about the death of that
unborn babe. Nay, as I said, she would go on about
nothing but George an' his gamekeeper job. What he
did. Was it by day and by night? Did he meet with many
poachers? Did he have a gun? Had he been shot at
himself? On and on, till my head were whirling wi' it.'

'I see. And she had just turned up at your door? On the last Sunday of last month? March the thirtieth, would it be?'

'If that were the last Sunday in March, it were then.'

A date that fitted.

'Right. And did she say at all why she was paying you this unexpected visit?'

'Nay. She said nowt about herself. An' that were a change, if you like. No, nowt but about what she were calling George's new job. Not that it were new. Six year he'd been gamekeeper for Colonel Timperley.'

'But she asked him all about his work? Do you remember anything she asked in particular?'

'Well, it's funny, now I think on it. But she were asking a lot about snares an' that. An' hardly any time's gone by when my George goes catching his foot in that snare right at the far end of his walk.'

But stolid Mrs Studley seemed not to make the connection.

As Harriet had. Cop Killer was not the bogeyman the *Evening Star*, and the nationals too, had been so eagerly painting. Cop Killer was definitely – catching out Dr Smellyfeet was a pleasure – a woman. A woman by the name of Grace Brown. Who had, some eight years ago, been injured in the eye by a police officer attending a violent demonstration outside an abortion clinic. And who, possibly in consequence, had lost the baby she had been carrying, possibly again at an age when she was unlikely to have been able to conceive another. Who, too, had been so badly affected mentally by this that she had been sectioned under the Mental Health Acts and had spent years in confinement. But who had recently been released. And then had started a campaign of revenge, long planned. Dr Smellyfeet was right there. A campaign that had started with a life for a life, the murder of wretched, innocent, rule-flouting PC Titmuss. Had then moved on, relentlessly, to the blinding and death of WPC Syed, another innocent. To the killing of Froggy Froggott and the wrenching away of one of his long yellow fangs. Then to the luring into the British Legion yard of young Mickey Chatterton, drugged and unable to resist till he had had his hand cut off and been left to bleed to death. And now on again to the killing of former PC George Studley, foot caught in a snare.

But that relentless career was not going to go one step further. No police officer was going to die in some fire, *burning for burning*. No police officer was going to be killed, *wound for wound*. No police officer was ever going to be somehow flogged to death, *stripe for stripe*. The Exodus litany was at an end.

The killer was Grace Brown, and within reach.

Chapter Nine

Only Grace Brown was not within reach. The identity of the *Evening Star*'s Cop Killer had been established, but the hunt turned out to be by no means at an end. Grace Brown had to be found. And she could not be found.

Mrs Studley had had no address for her, but Harriet had been sure there would be little difficulty in finding one. A single look at the Electoral Roll at City Hall might, she had thought, be enough. Or a discreet enquiry. Discreet, because it was important not to let Grace know that the police, whom the radio, the TV and the *Evening Star* daily described as hunting for a man, were aware the person they were seeking was a woman. However, neither the Electoral Roll nor a visit to the city Housing Department by DI Coleman produced a result.

And time, Harriet was only too aware, was not on her side. Grace Brown had fulfilled her maniac desire to kill a Birchester police officer by cutting off his foot, if in a less than perfect way. No – it was certain as night follows day – she would have set her sights on some other officer, to be killed *burning for burning*.

But, however much at her daily briefing Harriet

urged the investigation forward, there was an absurd, awkward fact they were up against. The name the detectives had been tasked with finding was Brown, the commonest in Britain. There were, they soon discovered, more than a thousand known Mrs Browns in Greater Birchester, even a few hundred solo Mrs Browns. Nor was it by any means certain Grace's name would be on any official lists. She could be living anywhere in Birchester. Even if she was within Dr Smellyfeet's psychological cup-shaped area centred on Queen Street still no record of her seemed to exist. Was she a temporary lodger somewhere? Or living almost anonymously in some hostel, under a different name? She could be sleeping rough, even. She was, after all, a discharged mental patient.

Tracing her through her stay in hospital under the Mental Health Acts, again discreetly avoiding saying why inquiries were being made, eventually proved a little more rewarding. There at last a trace of her was found. She had been admitted, as Harriet had worked out from Mrs Studley's not altogether precise recollections, eight years ago, and had been released *into the community*, as the authorities cheerfully said, shortly before Christmas something over three months ago. But almost at once she had left the address she had been registered at to disappear into the anonymity of the metropolis. Part of her well-thought-out plan, if Dr Smellyfeet's Profile had it right.

At Westholme Sergeant Franks, when Harriet had sharply questioned him, had agreed George Studley's shotgun had been lying on the ground as if pointing tauntingly at his foot-trapped body. But, as she had come to expect, no useful prints were found on the gun's triggers, nor anywhere else on its surfaces. Grace Brown, the planner, had left only the smudgy marks of gloves, marks so greasy that the Fingerprint Bureau had at once declared the gloves, like those that had left only smudges on the laser pen PC Wilkinson had picked up, had been much too thick and dirty for there to be any hope that, with all their most delicate techniques, they could raise even a few hopeful whorls.

So after *foot for foot* was there inevitably to come *burning for burning*? There could not be much doubt that the intent planning brain that had conceived the drugging of Cadet Chatterton and the killing of George Studley would be capable of contriving the death of some Greater Birchester Police officer in a fire somewhere. Perhaps a plan for it had been worked out well before young Mickey Chatterton had met his end. Perhaps plans for *wound for wound* and *stripe for stripe* were already lodged in the madwoman's head.

Harriet, with a groan, put in a call to Birchester's Chief Fire Officer. She told him she must be the first to know about any and every fire within the city boundaries. Even if her mobile rang every ten minutes.

The only good that had come out of at last knowing Grace's identity, she thought, was the quashing of a faint, unanalysable idea she had had, or had hardly had, that the mystery figure might be none other than Inspector Rob Roberts. As finder of the first body when he had claimed rather oddly to be out at that very hour just for a walk, he could have been, she now openly admitted to herself, Dr Smellyfeet's Mr Man. As Head of the Personnel Department he had had, in fact, access to the knowledge of where and even how PC Titmuss, Rukshana Syed and Froggy Froggott could be got at, as well as later Cadet Chatterton. And there had been, too, his prompt recitation of those damning words from the Book of Exodus. But the unexpected visit Grace Brown had made to her cousin had put a fat full-stop to all such half-thought thoughts.

Abruptly then the recollection of Rob producing that rolling Bible indictment there at her house sheltering from that shower under the veranda porch, provided her with the solution to the minor mystery she had promised the Chief Constable to investigate as soon as the hunt was over, the leaking to the *Evening Star* of Sir Michael's *foul agenda*. Plainly, the one man knowing of it who was not in her sworn-to-secrecy team had been responsible. A blabbermouth, Rob Roberts. Given no direct order to keep silent about the link between the killings and the biblical list, he could in justice hardly be blamed for talking of it. And somewhere what he had said must have filtered through to ears-ever-open Tim Patterson.

One complication dealt with. And one error, her own, in not including Roberts in the strict order she had given about the Exodus link. But no point in breast-beating. Stick, unswervingly, to the real task.

Plenty of other complications remained. To be answered only when Grace Brown had been traced down. If before then she had not succeeded in putting her deadly seal on yet another Greater Birchester Police officer. *Burning for burning.*

The black-heavy thought of all the days ahead when her pursuit of Grace Brown might mean doing nothing more positive than picking up her mobile to be told of some chimney fire out in a suburb lit up again in a corner of her mind a tiny warning light. Something needing clearing up. Some part of her thinking grating at a small malfunction.

Got it.

Teeth thoughtfully biting underlip, she rang Dr Smellyfeet and asked him to come round, and by the time he appeared she had the bulging file of his Profile open in front of her.

'Listen,' she said, 'there's something here that doesn't gell. All this about your subject being such a planner.'

'An obsessive planner I said. Doesn't mean Grace is someone of obvious intelligence, if that's what you're getting at.'

'Oh no, I've grasped that factor, thank you. No, it's this. Why if Grace is such a planner, a looker-ahead for snags and difficulties, why did she kill poor old Froggy Froggott when and where she did? Think. She didn't wait till she could get at him in some out-of-the-way spot – and Froggy went wherever it occurred to him to go barging in – but she attacked him right outside his house on a public road. All right, as it so happened at that early hour no one came by. But anyone might have done, a milkman, an early jogger. Grace was even lucky that Mrs Froggott didn't look out of her window earlier than she did, wondering why she hadn't heard his car roaring off.'

'All right. Yes, point taken. And I think you'll find if you read my Profile carefully that I do say somewhere, if not particularly explicitly, that even obsessive planners don't always succeed in planning everything. Page seventy-five, I think, if you'll look.'

'Okay, be right if you must. But that doesn't affect my point. Grace can't always be a planning killer. She hardly was when she went for Froggy.'

'No. No, I grant you that. And I think I know why she did that, now you've brought it to my attention. I was questioning Detective Inspector Coleman the other day about any extra details he could remember from the scene of Superintendent Froggott's death, and he happened to mention how ironic it was that Mr Froggott had been saying in a Greater Birchester Radio interview just the evening before that the deaths of Constable Titmuss and WPC Syed could not possibly be connected. *The idea couldn't be more rubbish if it was fished out of a municipal waste-truck*, he'd remembered the words.'

So do I, Harriet thought. They hurt then. Stupid bastard, Froggy.

'So, you see—' she began.

'Yes, I see all right,' Dr Smellyfeet went pouncing on, 'Grace must have had access to a radio. When she heard her deliberate revenge against Greater Birchester Police was being ignored she would have felt impelled there and then to kill one more officer, and an important one. Mr Froggott sealed his fate, as you might say, at that very moment.'

'Oh, yes. And it's quite possible, too, I suppose, that if Grace had known her message had been understood, that she had taken a life for the life of her born-dead baby and an eye for the loss of sight she had suffered, she might have been satisfied then. And no other police officers would have died.'

'A sobering thought. But, let me point out, that in fact what you've just made plain actually makes my Profile stand up all the better. Grace Brown is now obsessive beyond any point of reason.'

'So at any moment that mobile on the desk here will ring with news of a fire and it will turn out that one more police officer has been killed?'

'No, it won't be at any moment. You won't hear more of Grace till she has planned this next move of hers down to the very last detail. Take it from me.'

But it needed only one day, as it turned out, for something more about Grace to come to light. How, Harriet had asked, had it happened that police records, gone through day after day from within hours of it being accepted that WPC Syed had been murdered *eye for eye*, had not turned up any papers relating to a rejected claim for compensation made by a Mrs Grace Brown? At Westholme Mrs Studley had talked about her cousin being in 'a rare taking' when she had failed to get compensation for an injury to her eye that had led to the loss of the life within her womb. So why had the searches found nothing?

She had spoken personally to every one of the searchers on her team, and in no gentle way. It was only when days later she located someone who had failed to find a records entry that should have glared out that the answer appeared. Rob Roberts had been the man who had missed Grace's name.

'I— I— Yes, I skipped past it. It was a simple mistake. It— It had never occurred to me that the person the papers were calling Cop Killer could be other than a man. When I was going through the records if I found a woman's name at the head of any document I— I just passed it over.'

She gave him a long look of barely repressed rage, half directed at herself.

'You realize what this might have meant? If I hadn't happened to go and see that man George Studley's widow, we might never have been able to put our hands on the woman who's been murdering, one by one, officer after officer of the Greater Birchester Police. And, let me tell you, you may have other deaths on your conscience yet.'

She turned on her heel and marched out.

The hard justified rebuke.

Leaving an utterly mortified Rob Roberts, Harriet found herself asking with renewed sharpness a question that had lain dormant in her mind while the hunt for the killer had been at its most urgent. How was it, if Roberts with all his knowledge of police personnel and routines was not after all the killer as she had half-thought, that Grace Brown, former mental patient, a woman without resources, lurking in the byways of the city, had got to know as much as a police officer with all the information from the Personnel Department files at his fingertips? Nothing she could think of produced even a shadow of an answer.

With a sigh of exasperation she turned to asking herself the more urgent simple question: where is Grace Brown? A question she had to avoid even thinking of at her daily press conferences. The only slight advantage she had over Grace was her not knowing she had been traced at Westholme and her identity was known. Try as she might to keep her answers to the milling pressmen as limited as possible – What do they know about crime? About policework? – she had to suffer moments too near to being humiliating for comfort.

Then, out of the blue at her Monday conference, came another disquieting question, one she had hoped she would not hear at all until Grace Brown was safely in a cell.

'Superintendent Martens, is the *Evening Star* correct in understanding that Cop Killer has now committed a fifth murder which the task force under your command has been unable to prevent?'

What has bloody Patterson got on to?

'What the *Evening Star* understands is hardly something I can comment on.'

'Can I take it that is an admission?'

'No, you cannot.'

'But then would you like to comment on the fact that you yourself recently visited the village of Westholme?'

'I can see no comment to make about that.'

Tubby little Sergeant Sumpter was pulling surreptitiously at her sleeve, worried stiff that his friends in the press would be upset by her abrasive attitude. She jerked her arm free.

'And I suppose you have no comment to make on the death at Westholme, reported in the *Evening Star*, of a gamekeeper who was shot after his foot was trapped in a snare?'

'I understand there is to be a post-mortem in that

case. Until the results are to hand no one in the Greater Birchester Police can possibly say anything.'

'But do you agree that the death could be the work of Cop Killer? That the murder of Mr George Studley, a former officer of Greater Birchester Police, can be put down as one on the biblical list, *foot for foot?*'

A sharp buzz of thwarted interest now from the less well-informed reporters at the words *former police officer.*

Harriet grimaced in fierce vexation. And instantly regretted it. Two TV cameras had their vicious little red lights on.

'I think the *Evening Star* is putting two different twos together and hoping they can be presented as making four. Not for the first time.'

Another tug from Sergeant Sumpter.

Harriet repressed an impulse to turn and deliver him a public rebuke.

'I don't know about your arithmetic, Superintendent,' Tim Patterson lunged on. 'But in mine when you add this to Cop Killer's four murders, each plainly linked to words from the Book of Exodus, you get only one answer. Do you recall those words, Superintendent? The *Evening Star* jogs your memory from time to time, doesn't it?'

'That is a matter that I cannot possibly comment on at this stage.'

It was the best she could do. She slapped her two hands down on the big table with below its rank of microphones pointing at her, shot to her feet, turned sharply away and marched out.

Why the hell have I got to deal with bloody buzzing

mosquitoes like Tim Patterson, she thought, when at any moment I may be told some police officer somewhere in Birchester had been burnt to death. *Burning for burning.* The command from the Book of Exodus must be thrusting and throbbing inside Grace Brown's demented head.

She envisaged her there, sitting tensely, face contorted in concentration, plotting and plotting how, despite the fact that everywhere in the city police officers were going about in inseparable pairs, she could still entrap one of them into a place where they could be burnt to death. But where was the *there* where Grace was to be found? For all the confirmation Inspector Roberts' records had at last provided of her attempt to gain compensation for her eye injury, matters had hardly been advanced. Her address at the time she had made her claim – rejected as being not the result of police action – was where she and her former husband had lived. But she had left the house to go into the mental hospital eight years ago, and her husband had sold it soon after. Not surprising that such former neighbours as could be located had no newer address.

Gone to ground. Nowhere to be found. And plotting and planning, planning and plotting.

Chapter Ten

Next day Harriet had to swallow the bitter pill of seeing all over the front page of the *Evening Star* the sprawling headlines *Cop Killer Strikes Again – The Corpse Caught By The Foot*. The story below, after saying the victim was a former policeman, George Studley, now a gamekeeper, went on to point out the significance of his being trapped by his foot in a snare he knew nothing of. The Exodus list, too, was back in its full glory on Page One. And, turning with reluctance to the inside pages, she found a leader stating the question of police incompetence was being raised in 'concerned quarters'. And, worse, she had to acknowledge that the paper's story was correct in every detail. Bar the fact that it said the murder had been committed by a man.

But for how long, with detectives scouring Birchester looking for a Mrs Grace Brown, could the fact that they knew the sex of the demented murderer they were searching for be kept from getting to her own ears? For how much longer could they retain that small advantage?

Half-expecting her mobile to squeal with the report of yet another fire, Harriet was caught on the hop when a little after midday it was her phone that buzzed.

When she picked it up she heard the familiar *The Chief Constable for you, Superintendent*. It turned out, however, that, though she had plenty of troubles to contend with, at least Sir Michael was not one of them.

'Thank you for your memo about the Book of Exodus leak, Miss Martens,' he said at once. 'I suppose Inspector Roberts can hardly be blamed really. He hadn't been told after all that the information was to be kept confidential.'

'No, sir. But it should have occurred to him.'

'Well, I suppose so, but—'

'However, sir, there's worse to lay at Roberts' door. It was largely down to him that we failed to get on to Grace Brown through our searches of records of complaints made against the Force. It never occurred to him that complaints made by women were relevant.'

'I see. He just assumed, as we all did at that stage I'm afraid, that this individual was a man.'

'He's felt the rough end of my tongue, sir, over that. In no uncertain way.'

'Well, Superintendent, I've no doubt he's now throughly repenting his error. Which was after all understandable enough, and—'

'I beg to differ, sir. An error with such potential consequences is not understandable.'

'I take your point, of course. But Roberts is in the ordinary way a highly conscientious officer. Much laughed at, I understand, for his obsession with those files of his. An obsession which, from all that I hear at meetings with my fellow chief constables, has meant that the Greater Birchester Police personnel records are the envy of every other force. So I think you need take no further action.'

'If you say so, sir.'

But more irritating than any lack of vigour from above, she knew she would shortly have to sit listening once more at that afternoon's delayed press conference to its pundits wallowing in the aftermath of the *Evening Star* revelations. Which now she could hardly deny.

This time it was not Tim Patterson who led the attack but reporters from what she had always called mentally, and sometimes out loud, 'the gutter press'.

'Superintendent, is it true that the man who's been killing your officers one by one has struck again?'

The opening salvo. Avoiding action not worth attempting this time.

'I take it you're referring to the death of former Police Constable George Studley? If so, I have to tell you with deepest regret that our inquiries to date, though not yet complete, indicate that his death was in fact the latest in the series apparently dictated by certain words in the Book of Exodus.'

'You say your inquiries are not complete. When will they be, Superintendent?'

'When the post-mortem results are in my hands.'

'Not when you've arrested this man who's happily killing your officers?'

'That, too.'

Do absolutely nothing to turn face-up the one card still in my hands.

'And in the meanwhile, Superintendent, how long do you consider it will be before, in the words of the

Book of Exodus, one of your officers will be subjected to *burning for burning?*'

'A question I can hardly answer.'

'Superintendent,' another voice banging in, 'can you tell us what precautions you are taking to ensure the safety of police officers in Birchester?'

'If I did, I would be exposing them to greater danger.'

'Superintendent, has there been any suggestion that some more senior officer than yourself should be put in charge of the hunt?'

'Another question I'm unlikely to have an answer for. Are there any more?'

She was about to take advantage of the momentary silence among the media people to cut short the conference before any other malicious insinuations were made. But then she realized that, if she went, all she could do would be to go back to her office and sit waiting for Grace Brown to make her move, to attempt once again to kill.

Half out of her seat she sat back on to it.

'There is one thing I have to say.'

She saw the lenses of the TV cameras swing to point directly at her once again.

'In the past the conferences I have held have been little more than a battle of wits between us. You have put your questions, designed, frankly, to elicit some gaffe from me. And I have stonewalled. Time and again. But not without good reason. The fact is that a certain piece of information came into my hands which I considered not in the public interest to pass on. It is a fact about the identity of your Cop Killer that could well lead to their being arrested. I kept it secret because I did not want our target to know Greater Birchester Police were aware of it. They could have taken precautions to avoid being seen. However, too much fruitless time has gone by. I am ready now to take the risk.'

She could feel the tension mounting over her like a great overhanging wave, spume-flecked with sharp demands waiting to be made.

'The fact is,' she announced, 'that we now know that the person we are seeking in connection with the murders of police officers in Birchester is a woman. I ask for the co-operation of the public in apprehending one Mrs Grace Brown, of unknown whereabouts.'

Back at her office, half furious with herself, half glad to have at least taken a decisive step, she found Rob Roberts waiting for her. He appeared to be listening with grave sympathy to toothy Marjorie's latest woes.

Christ, he's not come bringing John's old mac back? As a bloody peace offering? Typical.

But it was a peace offering of another sort that Inspector Roberts had for her as she preceded him into her room.

'I hadn't realized you had a press conference, ma'am. But they told me I could wait for you up here.'

'That's all right. But what do you want? You haven't come to apologize once more, have you?'

A rueful smile below his big fair, fluffy moustache.

'No. No, ma'am. Though I suppose you could say in a way that I have.'

'Look, I've got a lot to get on with, and to tell you the

truth my temper's none too good after being baited by those ignorant idiots of reporters, so why don't you spit it out, whatever it is, and let me get on with it?'

An extra reddening in his ruddy cheeks.

'Yes, ma'am. Well, it's this. When you left me back in my office yesterday I began to wonder how I could put myself in the right again. What you said to me really went home. And then I thought: what's the worst problem facing you yourself at the moment? Is it anything I could somehow help to put right?'

'Inspector—'

The tone of her voice was enough.

'Yes. Sorry. Well, the first thing that came to me was that there was something in the Book of Exodus that sort of— Well, sort of cast light on it all.'

'Well?'

'So— So I went and looked it up. I still have the Bible I was given at Sunday School, and—'

'I hope this is going to be relevant.'

'It is, ma'am, it is. Listen. I've learnt it by heart. *If men strive, and hurt a woman with child, so her fruit depart from her, and yet no mischief follow he shall surely be punished, according as the woman's husband will lay upon him; and he shall pay as the judges determine. And if any mischief follow, then thou shalt give life for life.* That's where that list begins, ma'am. *Life for life, eye for—*'

'All right, what you've said actually goes some way to confirm that the person we're hunting, whose identity as one Grace Brown I've just made known to the media, is a woman and that she did lose a baby she was carrying. But I don't need to have that Exodus rigmarole thrown at me any more than the sodding *Evening Star* does every bloody day.'

'No, ma'am, no. I just thought it sort of indicated that Cop Killer might be acting because his wife lost a child. Only it seems you've known all along Cop Killer's a woman. So, well . . . Well, that wasn't too helpful. But, ma'am, I think I've also hit on something . . . Well, something even better. I think.'

'For heaven's sake, man. Either say it or bloody well shut up.'

'Yes, ma'am. Well, you see, it seemed to me that the question you must really want answering was: how did Cop Killer get to know so much about the Force? As much as I do, I thought. So then— Well, then it occurred to me they might, in fact, be— Well, just simply someone in the Queen Street nick somewhere. A civilian, of course. And, well, I've got access in Personnel to the records of everyone in the building, and I gave them a thorough search, men, women, everyone. It could have turned out to be one of the civilian clerks. But it wasn't. I'd worked out, in fact, that she probably was the Grace Brown you were referring to.'

'You're telling me you've found out how Grace Brown knew all she did? You're telling me that? Then spit it out, man. Spit it out.'

'Yes, ma'am. Yes. She— She, well, she worked in the canteen.'

'Worked? You said *worked*? She's not there still?'

'No. No, ma'am. She walked out, as I understand it, the day before Titty Titmuss – er – PC Titmuss, was stabbed, though . . .'

Harriet's thoughts leapt from point to point.

'Yes,' she said. 'It all hangs together. What was she in the canteen? Just someone collecting up dirty dishes? Scraping plates before they go into the washing-up machines?'

'Yes, just that, ma'am.'

'Right then. She'd know what that idler Titmuss was like, if only from what the others would say as soon as his back was turned. I wouldn't be surprised if there were jokes about his favourite place for a crafty drag.'

'There were, ma'am. I heard them once when I happened to be over in Queen Street.'

'And, of course, she'd know Syed had set up in that flat with her window-cleaner. Something like that's going to get talked about. And no doubt she'd know the girl rode there on her bike at the end of each day. And, as for Superintendent Froggott, his early start at his desk was legendary in his B Division days and lots of people would know he lived out at Boreham. So she'd be as well informed about him as— And, Christ, yes. You said it was just your understanding that she left the day before she killed PC Titmuss. But you sounded doubtful, right?'

'Well, yes. Yes, I was, a little. Someone said he'd seen her at work later than that. But—'

'Of course they did, whoever they were. She came back to get hold of young Chatterton or someone like him. It'd be perfectly easy. No one takes too much notice of a canteen worker, going round the tables stacking up used dishes, not if they keep themselves quiet. While keeping their ears open. No, it's obvious. She came back to the canteen, pretending she was still working there. She looked about her. She may have

123

needed to come for two or three days before she saw someone suitable. But then she spotted Chatterton, ideal for her, almost certainly sitting with some drink or other, tea, Coke. She had her Roofie ready – you can buy them in the pubs easily enough – and she dropped it into the lad's glass or cup and then contrived to lead him out. The British Legion Club's not so far from the Queen Street nick. It wouldn't be difficult.'

'You must be right, ma'am.'

'I am. I know it.'

Rob Roberts had the address Grace Brown gave when she got her canteen job, in Sullivan Street, a short row of terrace houses, once dignified enough, now in decline, a few minutes' walk only from Queen Street police station. Barely quarter of an hour later Harriet and a team of detectives, cars' sirens howling, tyres screeching at every corner, were there.

Grace Brown was not.

Each of the rooms in the just-this-side-of-re-spectable house had long been separately let, pro-vided with a Yale lock and a gas-meter on the landing outside. As soon as Grace's door had been forced, it was plain that she had deserted the place in a hurry. An old copy of the *Evening Star* was lying on the floor, in as much of a shapeless muddle as the copy with the head-line *An Eye For An Eye* that Marjorie had come wailing with into the office. There was a meal of sorts laid out ready to eat on the scratched surface of the room's one rickety table. Evidently Grace before starting it had heard the Greater Birchester Radio report put out immediately after the press conference at which she had been named, and had left, grabbing up just what she could snatch.

Had left perhaps only four or five minutes earlier. To disappear once again into the maze of the city.

Harriet put out a call for an immediate search of the area, but she had little hope it would be successful. Grace Brown, named or unnamed, was too cunning to be so easily caught. However, the team's search of her room swiftly brought to light at the bottom of the narrow old wardrobe, the cramped room's only other piece of furniture besides the bed, something well worth gaining possession of. A pair of carpenter's pincers with traces of blood visible on them still.

'Poor old Froggy,' the man who had found them said as, dropping them carefully into a tamper-proof evidence bag, he showed them to Harriet.

'Detective Superintendent Froggott,' she snapped at him.

'Yes, ma'am. Sorry, ma'am. I just . . .'

'Then don't *just*.'

'No, ma'am.'

She turned to the rest of the team.

'What are you hanging about for? Get to it. Every inch of this place turned over. Every inch.'

But it needed less than a minute more to retrieve a find even more valuable than the pincers that had tugged that long yellow tooth out of Detective Superintendent Froggott's mouth. Under the bed, pushed there as if it had been a pair of discarded slippers, was the stolen butcher's cleaver that had hacked off Cadet Chatterton's hand. An object that had surfaced in Harriet's imagination time and again since she had seen the boy's body. She watched it slipped into an evidence bag with a sigh of relief.

For a quarter of an hour more she stood watching the search team, although nothing of obvious significance came to light. At last she decided to go.

'Remember,' she said to the bent backs of the hands-and-knees searchers, 'I want anything that gives the slightest hint of where she may have gone to from here. If it turns out that something's been missed, you can look to going the rounds with a City Council tow-away vehicle.'

Nothing more was found however. It was clear before long that there would be nothing to find. Grace Brown's room – she had had it ever since she had left the 'halfway house' she had been directed to when she had been released from the mental hospital – had plainly been merely a refuge to hide in while she began on her demented revenge for what she believed Greater Birchester Police had done to her. *Life for life. Eye for eye. Tooth for tooth. Hand for hand. Foot for foot.*

And now to come – but when? – there would be *burning for burning*.

One by one the days went by, and the call that Harriet awaited, *Superintendent, two officers on patrol . . . burnt to death,* failed to come. A week passed.

Then Dr Smellyfeet – or Peter, as she had eventually agreed to call him – said he wanted to see her.

'Look, Harriet, I don't think there's anything more I can do here. I've added what I can to the Profile from what I've seen in that room of Grace Brown's, and that, honestly, isn't very much. I still think – bar getting it wrong about the sex of Cop Killer – that the bulk of what I said then holds true. I know it doesn't seem to have been positively helpful—'

'It hasn't been.'

'Yes. All right, you're not one to mince your words. And I agree, up to now, I certainly haven't helped you to locate that woman. But I still think in the end my findings may pay off.'

'Inside the magic circle, is she?'

'Well, she could still be, couldn't she? Inside it, or somewhere near its edge. I mean, you haven't been able to cover all the ground, have you? And she could be shifting from place to place within it. She could be living rough anywhere inside that line I've drawn. But I still give it as my professional opinion, based on more than a few cases, remember, that you'll find her eventually where she needs to be, where she can hardly help but be, inside her stamping ground. She will be within a quarter of a mile of that room of hers. I know it.'

'And you think we will find her? After almost a week's searching has got us nowhere, using every man and woman in the Force I can lay my hands on? I've got patrols out day and night tasked specifically with looking for a tall old woman probably wearing a long green or brown dress with a blue woolly hat on her head. It's not the best of descriptions, is it?'

'No. And I'm afraid I'll have to knock down the best bit of that. That hat. I rather think that Grace wears that hat only when she's out getting her revenge. It's ridiculously conspicuous, after all. If you've had every police officer in Birchester going about with that hat as a description, one of them would surely have spotted it long ago. I mean, Grace can't stay in hiding wherever she is all day and every day. She has to eat, if nothing else. And, remember, she's a planner, one of nature's planners. She'll have been able to work out that she would make herself far less conspicuous by simply taking off the blue hat that's pretty well her trademark.'

'Well, thank you for that. So I've even less of a description now. Practically all I've got is what ex-PC Studley's wife managed. That and what little the sharp-eyed members of Greater Birchester Police noticed about an old woman creeping round the B Division canteen collecting up dirty dishes and keeping her mouth tight shut. Which is damn-all. You know nobody at that room of hers either saw her more than once or twice? And remembers nothing about her? Your planner planned that all right. No wonder we're looking for a needle in a bloody haystack.'

'Well, if anyone can find her, you will, I'll say that.'

'Thanks for nothing. But, tell me – this is something I've been thinking this past day or two – isn't it possible Grace has simply given up? Isn't it possible she's decided the game's no longer worth the candle? That she's upped sticks and is God knows where now? In Scotland? Down in London? In some miserable seaside place somewhere?'

'No.'

Dr Smellyfeet, Peter, sounded as definite as she had ever heard him.

'No?'

'You've read my Profile, can you—'

Harriet smiled ironically.

'I read the Profile of someone you chose to call Mr Man.'

'Right, right. I got that wrong. But, don't forget, the statistics of serial murder were fully in my favour. It's just that we've got here the one who goes against the statistics. Still, that doesn't invalidate what I said. Grace Brown is as much a planner as was my Mr Man. She's the same person. And a person fundamentally is always what that person is. So, no, Grace has had a plan in her head, and she's going to carry it out. The silence you're getting now is, in fact, simply proof of that. She's planning a *burning for burning* killing. Lulling you and your searching officers into relaxing vigilance is all part of that plan. I simply haven't any doubt of that.'

'All right. How long do you say Grace is willing to hide, wherever she is, and take no action?'

'Ah, if I knew. If I had anything to indicate what that answer might be. But I haven't. And that's why I asked to see you.'

'Oh, yes, you're wanting to go back to your academic retreat.'

'Well, I am. I have commitments. I've a career to keep on the rails. I see nothing wrong in that. And if circumstances change here, I'm at the end of the phone.'

'Okay. I suppose it's true, you aren't contributing all that much any more. Which, in fact, doesn't mean to say that you haven't contributed something. The Police Authority has had its money's worth. More or less.'

'But you, you're happy to see the back of me?'

'As I said, your usefulness has come to an end, at least for the time being.'

'Thank you. But let me say before I go that I've been impressed, much impressed, with the way you've led this inquiry. It's been a hard road, a bloody hard road. But I don't think anyone else would have travelled it any better.'

'Thank— No, there is one thing more you might be able to do.'

'Ask.'

'Once before I put a proposition to you. And, if this wait goes on much longer, I'll be tempted to put it into practice.'

'I think I can guess what you're going to say.'

'Then tell me.'

'Well, am I right? Is it that you're thinking once more of issuing some sort of direct challenge to Grace Brown?'

Chapter Eleven

Dr Scholl had been even more dismissive than before of the idea of any sort of person-to-person challenge flushing out Grace Brown. Despite his facing-both-ways answer when Harriet had first suggested the notion, *Sir Michael would never agree*, he was now more direct.

'No, Harriet. No. It would be taking an intolerable risk. You're dealing with a severly disturbed individual. It's not like trying to guess which way some common-or-garden criminal will jump, and perhaps giving a push in one direction or the other. No, there's no telling what someone like Grace Brown would do if you faced her with any sort of challenge. It could drive her to even greater lengths than she has gone to so far.'

'I'd say she's gone as far as it's possible to go already. She's killed five people, damn it. Five police officers. Five of my colleagues, good or bad. And she's threatening more. *Burning for burning*. If it would put a stop to that . . . As it is, I seem to do nothing but take calls from the Fire Service, thinking each one's going to say a police officer's been burnt alive.'

'All right, some sort of a challenge might bring that to an end. But equally it might not. It might result in not just one police officer being burnt to death but – heaven knows – dozens somehow.'

'Okay, you've given me your view. Now, no hard feelings, but bugger off back to cosy academia.'

Nevertheless, as another week went slowly by with neither any sign of where Grace Brown might be hiding nor anything even indicating that her plan to kill some police officer by burning had been tentatively put into operation, Harriet did not forget the blackly unorthodox notion that had occurred to her. So on the Saturday when the Chief Constable telephoned – his calls were no longer daily affairs – after she had reassured him that every precaution was still being taken to safeguard his officers she ventured to broach the subject.

'Sir Michael, it's been represented to me that it's not enough simply to wait for Grace Brown to act. We ought, it's been said' – she lied unblushingly – 'to make an active move. In short, the suggestion is to issue her, not with an appeal, but with a challenge. A challenge to meet me myself somewhere, face to face.'

'I hope you took no notice of such a suggestion, Superintendent. Just think what that wretched rag the *Evening Star* would make of a stunt of that sort. Who was it who put such a crazy idea to you?'

Some quick thinking.

'As a matter of fact, sir, it was the *Evening Star*, or at least that crime reporter of theirs, Tim Patterson.'

Who, as the Chief Constable's *bête noire*, would hardly be likely to be asked to confirm or deny the invention.

'Yes. The sort of thing I might have expected from a young man of his sort. Anything for a sensation.'

'I simply thought I ought to hear your view, sir. I have. You see it as a stunt. That's the end of the matter.'

But even the *Evening Star*, Harriet realized at lunchtime when Marjorie came trotting in with the new edition, had quietly dropped altogether its panel listing the unyielding justices of the Book of Exodus. Its pages now were filled with reports of crimes, major and minor, mostly committed in the area of Birchester policed by B Division.

> *Drug Deals on Our Doorstep – Residents Complain*
> *Youths' Assault on Girl, 16*
> *Four Homes in One Street Raided*
> *Black Youth Stabbed*
> *Six Attack White Youth*

She began to find herself every now and again actually wanting to be quit of the responsibility she had been proud to be given and to be back again running *Stop the Rot*, putting as many wrongdoers as possible into the cells or making them wish in other ways that they had never embarked on the criminal life. How much better it would be than chasing a ghost, as she had begun to think of Grace Brown.

But she never for a moment really contemplated asking the Chief Constable to relieve her. Grace Brown was not in custody, and it was her task to see that she was. All right, Grace might not even be in Birchester any more, let alone inside Dr Smellyfeet's mis-shaped circle. She might be anywhere. But equally she might be somewhere within reach. And if so she must be found and put out of the way of causing harm.

At her briefings every morning, weekdays and weekend, she reiterated this message.

'All right, another twenty-four hours gone by and none of you have seen anything or heard anything of Grace Brown. For your sakes I hope it wasn't for want of trying. Let me remind you once again, look at those words I wrote on this board here at the start of our hunt. That list from the Book of Exodus. And it's being worked through. Four of your fellow officers murdered by this woman, as well as a man who had served his time in the police. Number one, PC Titmuss stabbed to death on night patrol, *life for life.* Number two, WPC Syed sent to her death under a bus blinded by a laser pen, *eye for eye.* Number three, Detective Superintendent Froggott, again, stabbed to death, with a tooth wrenched from his head, *tooth for tooth.* Number four, Cadet Chatterton lured to his death, his right hand hacked off, *hand for hand.* Number five, former police constable, Mr George Studley, leg caught in a snare, shot and then left to bleed to death, *foot for foot.'*

She looked round the big room. Nothing but sombre, intent faces.

'All right, it's possible that the mad killer we're looking for has given up on her perverted revenge. But let me say aloud, once again, the remainder of those words from the Book of Exodus.' She pointed to the list, already beginning to fade on the whiteboard. *'Burning for burning, wound for wound, stripe for stripe.* The whole probability is that Grace Brown means, if she can, to get to the end of her list, that she's still here, here in Birchester, hiding and plotting. But every now and again she must be having to venture out into the streets. And there we'll get her. All right, we've still not got a really good description. Dr Scholl thinks it's certain the one useful thing we thought we had, the shapeless blue woollen hat she was seen wearing, is something she puts on only when she is out intent to kill. And, another minus, we do know it's not obvious that she's blind in one eye. The people at the mental hospital told us that. But despite all that, we can get her. And we will.'

But in private she went so far one afternoon as to phone Dr Scholl at his university and put to him again, hoping against her better judgement he would now agree, the notion that Grace could have abandoned her vendetta.

'I hear you, Harriet. And I still have to say, unless you have some real evidence to the contrary, that Grace must be in Birchester. Read my Profile. That woman is a dyed-in-the-wool planner. And when I use that expression, believe me, it's not just a convenient cliché. I mean it: her habit of planning everything she does is an engrained part of her personality, unaffected by the fixation she's now prey to. And, remember, it isn't that someone of that personality-set needs to possess a high-achieving intellect. Grace Brown is not, I believe, particularly intelligent. But she has plenty of cunning. You don't have to be intelligent to be a planner. Just someone who can't help planning. And it's my unchanged opinion that even now she is planning to burn to death a member of the Greater Birchester Police.'

'Okay, that's what you think. But I'll make no bones about it. I've a very strong suspicion I'm wasting my time sitting here in this office now. When I think of the work I was doing before this madwoman stuck her knife into that slack fool Titmuss I feel doubly frustrated. I could be back there in B Division, the worst area of Birchester, clamping down on the criminals from drug dealers to public urinators, making them realize there's right and wrong in this world—'

'Harriet, listen. Once or twice when I was up there in Birchester, more than once or twice actually, I wondered whether I ought to raise that subject with you.'

'What subject, for heaven's sake?'

'The subject of your much-heralded *Stop the Rot* campaign. Only I didn't want anything to interfere with the co-operation I felt there should be between us.'

'You had objections to *Stop the Rot*?'

'I didn't say so.'

'But you meant it. All that not wanting to spoil co-operation between us. I sussed out your flattery technique, Peter, before you'd been in my office ten minutes.'

'Yes. Well, yes, I do actually believe a certain amount of flattery is necessary to secure co-operation with police officers when I'm brought in on a case. You people are such believers in your own limited methods. Anything I can do to soften you up before I put to you the sort of conclusions I know I am going to reach is worth trying.'

'All right. You tried to soften me up. You failed. But when you did put your conclusions about your Mr Man to me, you can't say I didn't listen.'

'My Mr Man, how much does that indicate you listened?'

'Okay, I take that back. But I did listen, didn't I?'

'You did. And that's why I'm going to say to you what I hesitated to say when the hunt for Grace Brown was at its most urgent. And that's this. I don't think your approach to criminal or delinquent members of the public, or even to social incompetents, is the right one. When Sir Michael rang me up and asked me to come and see what I could do, he said you had been put in charge of the inquiry. I knew your name, of course. There'd been stories in the papers about you and your so-called zero tolerance policing. And I hesitated to agree to come then because I foresaw an absolute difference of opinion between us about how police operations should be conducted. But I did come. The case was too fascinating.'

'The case was going to get your name in the papers, don't you mean?'

Down the line came the sound of a heavy sigh.

'All right, Harriet, what if I admit that I find it pleasant, agreeable, what you will, to find my efforts to assist bringing dangerous criminals to justice bring me renown, fame, whatever. But that doesn't mean that my efforts are invalid.'

'Have I ever suggested they were?'

'Yes, you have. From time to time. But you've also admitted that they were to some extent at least helpful to you. So that's why I've held my tongue.'

'Then I suggest you no longer need to exercise such restraint.'

'Very well then, I won't. Let me put it this way. Even reading about you in the necessarily trivialized pieces in the papers, before I had met you at all, I was alienated by your attitude of always being right. And when I did meet you there were many occasions when I had to check the antipathy that same attitude had aroused in me. Almost your very first words to me – I recall them distinctly – were that you weren't expecting any help from me. Your mind was made up.'

'Yes. It was. You don't get anywhere in this life unless you've decided where you're going, and you go.'

'You make my point for me. And I won't deny that at times that's a useful way of going about things. I suppose your insistence that the person I called Mr Man was a woman is a case in point. You believed you were right and scarcely paid any attention to the other point of view. Okay, you were correct, as it happened. But you very well might not have been. The facts were against you.'

'Except the last fact of all, that Mr Man was a woman.'

'There you are. Saying *I'm right* once more.'

'I was right.'

'Yes, but you can't be right every time. That's just what I objected to in your attitude to policing your area of Birchester. That you applied the same rigid rule to every criminal of every sort you encountered, and, worse, you ordered the officers under you to do the same. People are different, Superintendent. You ought to realize that, and pay attention to it.'

'No, Dr Sm— No, Peter, at the fundamental level people are not different. They're either right or wrong, and if they're wrong then I'm going to point it out to them, as hard as I should do. It's no use you and your softy friends saying there's always some excuse for criminal behaviour. There isn't. There's right, and there's wrong. And I know which is which, if no one else does.'

'Harriet, I know how effective that attitude of yours has been in putting an end to a great deal of anti-social behaviour, but—'

'No buts about it. You say you know my actions have ended what you like to call *a great deal of anti-social behaviour*. But let me tell you in fact what they have done. I launched *Stop the Rot* eighteen months ago, soon after I was appointed to B Division. In its first year crime was cut by thirty-one per cent. A fact. In the first month of the operation burglaries in the area were cut from over four hundred to less than two hundred. Another fact. My team in that first month stop-searched over a thousand people more than in the month before we began. And one in ten of those stops resulted in convictions. For offences that were going to result in harm to the public. We brought safety back to the streets. That's another fact.'

'All right, all right. No one's denying that you produced astonishing results. But that's not my point. My point is that you did it in a dangerous way. You did it by assuming you were the one who knew best all along the line.'

'Someone has to know best. Someone, in this murky world, has to open their eyes and see right from wrong.

And it so happens that in Birchester here and now – or rather not now but yesterday, yesterday damn it – I was that one. It wasn't easy for me. Don't think it was. But it was there to be done, and I did it. I had to.'

She had slammed down the phone then.

And – the thought was ringing in her head now – she would say again to anybody who asked for it every word she had said then. And mean them.

Chapter Twelve

As day followed day with no sighting of Grace Brown nor reports of any activity that might be put down to her, Harriet began almost to be convinced that she might not be anywhere in Birchester. Despite the confident assertion in Dr Smellyfeet's Profile, often open on her desk, that a psychological planner would not abandon a plan, more and more frequently she pictured to herself a tall, gaunt, oldish woman, striding the streets of some pre-season, cut-prices seaside resort, the spring gale-whipped breakers crashing down on the promenade at her feet. Even perhaps contemplating throwing herself into the turbulent, foam-flecked sea.

But she did not, as she had had half a mind to do before she had had her row on the telephone with Peter Scholl, advise the Chief Constable to rescind the order that no uniformed officer was to go on to the streets of Birchester unaccompanied by another.

If I'd asked Smellyfeet then, she thought, and he'd said the order ought to be kept in force, almost certainly I'd have got it cancelled.

The notion whined for a moment like an irritating mosquito in her head.

And came whining there again, more than once, as

the days went by. Until at the start of the following week, when still nothing had happened even to indicate that Grace might have tried to lure some police officer to death by fire, she began to think the time was coming when the loss from restricting policing would outweigh the possible danger of losing one more officer.

It was a visit from Inspector Roberts that finally tipped the scales.

'There's something I think I ought to say, ma'am. You know, I see it as part of my duties to bear in mind the welfare of members of the Force. And— And— Well, I know it's important that—'

'Inspector, say what you've got to say and get on with it.'

'Yes, ma'am. Well, it's simply this. A good many of the uniform constables are getting fed up with having to change into civvies night after night when they finish their reliefs and having to get into uniform at the start of their day in the cramped conditions of most nicks in the city. And— And it's worse for the women, so they tell me.'

His naturally ruddy face visibly darkened in a blush.

Soft fool.

'All right, Inspector. You've made your point, and if there's been dissatisfaction you're right to report it. But I didn't ask for that order to go out just for fun. Officers' lives were at risk, and still are, and they should be damn glad I remember it.'

'Yes. Yes, ma'am. Well, I— I'll tell anyone else who complains what you've said.'

'Will you, Rob? Or will you give them the soft-speak version?'

He was making for the door, plainly attempting to get out of having to provide an answer to that, when another question occurred to her.

'Oh, and, Rob, tell me something that's been nagging at me ever since you discovered Titmuss's body in that disused passageway.'

A look of apprehension.

'Just what were you doing there at that very early hour? Don't tell me it was because of your urgent need for an early paper.'

He stood there in the doorway, an absolute illustration of the term *hangdog*.

'Well?'

'It was— I was— Well, to tell you the truth, I'd— I'd had a bit of a row with my wife. I— I just had to get out of the house.'

'I might have guessed. Okay, on your way.'

A police officer in retreat after a skirmish in the battle of the sexes. Rather him . . .

But, reviewing all the pros and cons of double-officer policing after Rob Roberts had managed at last to close the door between them, in the end she phoned the Chief Constable.

'Sir, about not permitting officers in uniform to go out on the streets except in pairs.'

'Yes, Miss Martens, I've been considering that matter. The loss of patrolling hours is having a measurably bad effect on the crime figures. Not to speak of the overtime hours accumulating.'

'No doubt, sir. And there's another factor. From

things that have been coming to my ears, I gather morale's being affected as well. Changing in and out of uniform adds to the time officers are on duty, besides the discomforts of changing in restricted spaces in some of the smaller stations.'

'Yes. Yes, I'm glad you've drawn my attention to that aspect. So, are you thinking that, with nothing being heard of that mad woman, we could safely withdraw the order?'

'Yes, sir. I am. It may be exposing officers to some risk, but plainly it's much less than when you issued the order, sir.'

'Some risk . . . Yes. Perhaps after all . . .'

'No, sir. You can't be a member of the cloth without the possibility of facing danger. It may be, to an extent, a hard decision. But I think it's one that's got to be taken.'

'Very well, Superintendent. Shall we say normal policing to be resumed from six a.m. tomorrow?'

'Yes, sir.'

And next day, just after darkness had fallen, there came a buzz on her direct-line phone.

'Detective Superintendent Martens here.'

'Miss Martens.' She recognized the voice: the Fire Service one she had heard so many times already. 'We've had a call to a house fire in Batley Street. A sudden—'

'One moment, Mr Wythenshaw. My red phone's buzzing.' She picked it up. 'Yes?'

'A fire in a house in Batley Street, ma'am, and there's— There's a uniform officer inside. They think—'

144

'Never mind what they think. I'll be there in less than ten minutes.'

She was there within that time. As her car swerved into the narrow street in the run-down Chapeltown area, well within Dr Smellyfeet's cut-off circle, she saw the high white tongues of flame striking up towards the night sky. A fire engine had pulled up outside the blazing house and its crew were busy rolling out their hoses. Already a turntable ladder was being hoisted. A panda patrol car was parked opposite the burning house and half a dozen people from nearby were standing gawping.

Braking hard, she got out and ran.

Beside the panda a flat-capped constable was sagging over its bonnet, looking as if at any moment he would cover it in vomit. She strode across.

'You know me? Superintendent Martens. What happened?'

He raised his head an inch or two and gave her a white-faced, glazed look.

'My mate,' he brought out. 'My mate. Inside.'

'Stand to attention when you talk to me.'

He looked as if a strong electric shock had gone through him from feet to head. And jerked himself upright.

'Sorry. Sorry, ma'am.'

'I asked you what's happened.'

'Yes. Yes, ma'am. It— It's Constable Strachan. He's inside there. And— Jesus, I think he's being burnt alive.'

'Go on. I want to know exactly what happened.'

'Well, we— we were just driving down the street here. It's on our regular route. You often get druggies

145

here. Girls bring their clients. You can see what sort of a place it is.'

He gave a glance each way along the narrow terraced street, its littered pavements, doors and windows of half its houses boarded up, white-painted sprawled graffiti visible in the fire engine's arc lights. *Up United – Kill Police – Rovers Are Scum.*

'I know what sort of a place this is. I ran B Division until a few weeks ago. Tell me precisely what happened.'

'Yes. Well, just as we came along, right from the far end we saw a sudden outbreak of flame in the ground-floor window there. Not much, but definitely a fire. So we stopped.'

'Yes, yes. Go on.'

'Well, then an old gent opened the window on the floor above and called for help.'

'An old gent? You're sure it was a man? Sure?'

'Yes. Yes, of course, ma'am. He had a beard, long white. Sort of Father Christmassy.'

'So your mate went in to try and rescue him. That it?'

'Yes. Yes, it was. He said something about— About Cop Killer, *burning for burning* and that. But more as a sort of joke, like. Seeing that the order to go about in pairs had been rescinded, and this wasn't a woman but just an old man. And so he ran over to the house. He had to kick the door in, but that didn't seem to be difficult. And while he was doing it I radioed the Fire Service, ambulance and everything.'

'And then?'

'Well, that's when it began to go pear-shaped. Jock –

er – Constable Strachan, ma'am, went in, heading straight for the stairs in front of him. I didn't see any flames beyond the door. Nothing to be worried about. And then— Then I saw Jock suddenly disappear. I think the boards in the passage must have— Or they may have— Ma'am, they may have been taken away under the bit of carpet there. So he'd fall through. These houses have basements. He'd have fallen right down. And then— I don't know how it happened but all of a sudden the flames got worse. They sprang up, coming from the basement. A sudden whoosh of— Of white flames like you see there, ma'am.'

The wretched little house was almost all ablaze now. The eye-searing white flames leaping up in narrow tongues.

Two more fire engines, bells clanging, blue lights flash-flash-flashing, came to a halt beside the first. Harriet went across to the officer in charge, noticing as she got nearer the house an odour that reminded her, all too horribly, of summer garden barbecues. She blotted the thought from her mind.

'Detective Superintendent Martens,' she introduced herself. 'You know one of my men's inside there?'

'I do, Superintendent. And— Well, I have to tell you, you'll not see him again.'

'I guessed as much.'

She wrinkled her nose.

'Yes, it's an unmistakable smell. I hate it whenever I encounter it.'

'I dare say. But, tell me, what about the other one in there, an old man who called out from that window?'

She looked up at the flame-filled square that until a few moments before had been a dark rectangle.

'We've seen nothing of anyone up there so far. My chap on the ladder would've let us know if there'd been signs of life.'

'Do you know anything about these houses? Is there a way out at the rear?'

'Well, they're back-to-backs actually. And the terrace of the street beyond's in much the same state as this one, half the houses unoccupied and those that are – I'd take a bet on it – filled with squatters, all bar a few old inhabitants hanging on. No, I'd say it's almost certain the old fellow managed to get out that way.'

Old fellow? Or old but active woman? Harmless squatter? Or Grace Brown?

A second panda car came up to a brake-squealing halt.

Harriet went over.

'Don't waste your time here. Get round into the next street – Hartley Street, is it? – and see if anyone's made their way out through some empty house there. I don't doubt we're too late, but give it a try.'

'Then, ma'am, it's her? Cop Killer?'

'Just get round there.'

The car roared away.

'Superintendent Martens?'

From the ring of darkness round the brightly flame-illuminated area surrounding the burning house Tim Patterson came striding up. Ready as ever at the scene of the crime.

'Superintendent, tell me, is this Cop Killer striking? *Burning for burning*, Super?'

Harriet turned and went across to the panda that had not so long before come idly by on patrol. Its driver had got himself inside and was sitting gripping the wheel in front of him as if, were he not to, he would slump to the floor.

'Constable.'

'Ma'am.'

'Get out of the car. Just over there you'll see a young man who may be known to you, a Mr Patterson of the *Evening Star*. Escort him to the end of the street and tell him if he sets foot in it again he'll be charged with obstruction. Yes?'

'Yes, ma'am.'

A good deal steadier than he had been half a minute before, the constable obeyed.

Harriet watched until he had led the reporter, resentment squealing out of every inch of his hunched back, to the far end of the street.

A few moments later the second panda came in at the other end of the road. Its driver brought it to a halt within a few feet of Harriet.

'Ma'am, bad news.'

'She got away?'

'Yes, ma'am. If it was her. Old lady woken by the fire saw a woman come out of a derelict house two doors along from her and hurry away. Tall, she said, and with a darkish hat on her head. Black, blue, she didn't know. But it looks as if it could be Cop Killer all right. I radioed in straight away. Perhaps we'll pick her up yet.'

'Or perhaps not. The woman's a planner. She'll have planned her get-away.'

'Yes, ma'am. And there was a funny thing.'

149

'All right, tell me.'

'In the letter-box of the house she came out of, jammed in it, there was this, ma'am.'

He reached down beside him and presented Harriet with a full cotton-wool white beard with neat loops either side all ready for any Santa to hook round his ears.

'Yes, Constable, as I said, a planner. Just after Christmas – as long ago as that – beards like this would have been easy to get hold of.'

And so, she thought, perhaps Grace had intended all along to carry out the full list of rigid Exodus commands. It had been only a small change of plan to make Froggy Froggott her victim. But, all the same, it had been a change of plan. Grace not always a perfect planner. Hope here? The two last tragedies after all avoidable?

Nevertheless the Chief Fire Officer's eventual report on the Batley Street fire made bitter reading. Stripped of its verbiage, it said that the main seat of the blaze had been in the basement of the house from which the body of Police Constable Strachan had been recovered. The source of the flames was petrol, liberally puddled there. It had been ignited – the device had been easy to find – with a simple contrivance using an old electric fire with a wire running to a switch at the rear of the house. There had been, too, a second smaller fire, in the middle of the front room. But that had consisted simply of paper and a few sticks, easy enough to have put out with a bucket of water. And, finally, it was plain that floorboards in the narrow hallway had been removed beneath the carpet runner so that anyone hurrying in would be sent tumbling into the basement below.

Harriet sat, when she had finished reading, looking at the Santa Claus beard, now in a transparent evidence bag, that lay beside Dr Smellyfeet's Profile on her desk.

But will that wretched object ever have to be brought into court, she asked herself. To be used as part of a long complex of evidence in the trial of Grace Brown on six counts of murder? Six counts at present. But when, if ever, that trial is held will it be on seven counts? *Wound for wound?* On eight counts? *Stripe for stripe?* Three murders committed while newly promoted Detective Superintendent Harriet Martens had been in charge of the case. Two more still to be committed?

She picked up her phone and asked for the Chief Constable.

'Sir, I've just been reading the report on the fire that killed Constable Strachan. It confirms beyond doubt that it was as the result of a deliberately planned booby-trap. And, sir, I can only blame myself. It was on my direct advice that officers ceased going on the streets in pairs. A bad decision. The situation in effect was unchanged, and, whatever difficulties arose in keeping that original order, I ought not to have sanctioned the easy answer.'

'But, Miss Martens, no one's blaming you. It was a perfectly reasonable course of action to advocate, and one which I myself endorsed. Besides which, there were two officers together there in – what's the place? –

Batley Street. You cannot possibly take responsibility for what occurred then.'

'Nevertheless, I do, sir. All right, I know that, as it so happened, there were two men at the scene of that fire. But the one who was killed said, sir, that he didn't need to worry about going into the house on his own, as that order had been rescinded. I know he was under the impression he had an old man with a white beard to rescue' – she looked down once again at the trumpery, ear-hooked cottonwool-like mass in the evidence bag – 'but if that order had still been in force, wouldn't he have thought twice? Wouldn't he have gone in there with a degree of caution? Wouldn't he have avoided that simple trap in the hallway? He had the right to feel he was in no exceptional danger. And I ought to have known that any officer in uniform, at the very least, was still at risk from that woman. No, sir, I do blame myself, and if you wish to put the operation into someone else's hands, I'll be glad to accept that.'

Chapter Thirteen

Harriet, her offer to the Chief Constable made, did not make it again. She had said what she had to say. It was up to Sir Michael to accept or not. Sir Michael took a little time, and a good many words, to reply.

'Miss Martens, it was not without thought that I put you in charge of the inquiry into the deaths of three of my officers. And I know well it may be said in such places as the so-called editorials of that rag the *Evening Star*, and even in the national press, that since you have been in charge all that has happened is that there have been three more killings. But I cannot see that any action of yours, or any action omitted by you, could have saved those men, that lad. I have been aware of every step you took to prevent those deaths, and I am quite satisfied you could have done no more than you did. Including, let me say, your advising me that the weight of the argument was in favour of rescinding the order that sent our officers going about the city in pairs. So, no, Superintendent, I put you in charge, and I wish you to remain in charge.'

'Thank you, sir.'

Nevertheless, as Harriet put down the receiver, she made a resolution.

Plainly there was no point in asking Sir Michael, once again, if she could issue a personal challenge to Grace Brown. But were a challenge to be issued without her consent or authorization . . .

Another day, another press conference. As well attended as either of the ones since the murder of PC Strachan, but without any new questions called out. Harriet had stated the day after the fire in Batley Street that the blaze had every appearance of having been the work of Mrs Grace Brown, 'or Cop Killer, as you people like to call her'. No, she had answered then, no one had been arrested. At the next day's conference she had said that it was confirmed that PC Strachan had been lured into a trap at Batley Street and that 'we have no evidence to the contrary when we say we are looking for Grace Brown'. And, no, 'we do not at the present time have any indication of where she may be'.

She began now with a bare statement repeating the details of what the report on the fire had said.

'Am I right in understanding, Superintendent, that the order by which police officers in uniform did not go on to the streets alone was countermanded on your express instructions less than twenty-four hours before this new tragedy?'

'Not on my instructions, Mr Patterson, but certainly on my direct advice to the Chief Constable. Otherwise your information, however obtained, is accurate.'

'Wholly accurate?'

'Yes.'

'So do you accept any blame for having advised

the Chief Constable it was safe to rescind the original order?'

'Yes, I do.'

'And has the order that officers in uniform should go about in pairs been reinstated?'

'It has, with certain changes to the original. We regard the situation as exceptionally serious.'

'What changes would those be? Were they again made on your advice?'

'Naturally they were. It's my duty to keep the Chief Constable in touch with day-to-day policing as it affects the presence in Birchester of a woman dedicated to attacking his officers.'

'You haven't said what the changes are? Are police-women, for example, to be withdrawn from the streets altogether?'

'Certainly not. They are officers of Greater Birch-ester Police just like any other officers.'

'Well, then what changes have you made? Or advised, as you like to put it.'

'A few simple adjustments to ensure the city is policed to the best possible extent. Officers on traffic point-duty, for instance, at times when they are fully in the public view may be allowed to operate without a fellow officer beside them. That and a few similar relax-ations are all.'

One of the nationals jumped in.

'Am I right in thinking, Superintendent, that you're actively expecting as of now a murder of a police officer that fits the biblical exhortation *wound for wound*?'

'I am glad to find a member of the press has studied his Bible.'

Another national reporter, licking lips.

'And *stripe for stripe*, Superintendent? Are you taking measures to prevent one of Birchester Police's officers being flogged to death?'

'We are taking every precaution against every possible eventuality.'

-'Are you going to order women police officers to stay off the streets, then? Or are you prepared to see one of them whipped, *stripe for stripe*?'

'Do you really expect me to have it announced in the media what precise steps we are taking to ensure that the woman we suspect of murdering six police officers will not murder any more?'

About turn, and leave the room.

But not to return to the sanctuary of her office.

The quickest way to go from Greater Birchester Police A Division headquarters in Wellington Gardens to the offices of the *Evening Star* in King Street, Harriet knew, was through the dull, calm spaces of the gardens themselves, past their symmetrical flower-beds, now bright with tulips and polyanthus planted in circles of municipal regularity, on down a broad flight of shallow stone steps and at last round a large, railings-surrounded pond, its April waters black and chill.

As Tim Patterson, striding along bare-headed, lank dark hair flattened on his overlarge skull, big spectacles flashingly reflecting any rare glimpse of sunshine, light-coloured trench-coat flapping open, approached the pond, he came to an abrupt halt at the sight of

Harriet, standing apparently looking at three ducks aimlessly swimming.

Harriet, who seemed only to be looking in the direction of the ducks, permitted herself a tiny smile.

'Miss Martens, I'm surprised to find you here.'

She wheeled round.

'Mr Patterson.'

'Oh, call me Tim, for heaven's sake. It's not as if we don't know each other.'

'Well, yes, I suppose we do, though I'm surprised in my turn to find you wanting, as they say, to pursue the acquaintance.'

'Because of the put-downs you dish out to me all the time? Your stony-faced answers at your conferences? And the odd little jibe? Or your having me ordered out of Batley Street when all I was doing was reporting on that blaze? And even sending me about my business when PC Titmuss was stabbed and I was first on the scene? Well, you know, a reporter has to learn to ignore that sort of thing.'

'Oh yes, I've seen that ignoring's a lesson you've learnt, if only from the way you come up for more at each new conference.'

'Ah, but you never know, you see, when patience will get you what you want. I mean, like now. Mightn't there have been something this morning you could have said, but didn't? Perhaps because the nationals were gunning for you? But now that we're here, just the two of us with no one else about, can't you give me a hint? If only because we're both Birchester people.'

'You expect me to feed you titbits?' Harriet flared out.

And then bit her lip.

'Of course,' she said, 'there are things I could tell you. And I would, if I was a different sort of police officer.'

'Well, yes, I grant you that. You are different from most police officers I've had to deal with. Almost all of them are only too happy to give me a quote – old Froggott always was – whether in the middle of an investigation or whether it was outside the court when they'd managed to secure a conviction.'

'Well, you won't get any of that sort of crap from me. Telling the world that they've just put away *a truly evil man, a monster, someone bestial.* In my book, a police officer is there to enforce the law, not to tell the world that someone's better or worse than somebody else. You reporters ought to be ashamed to milk that sort of self-righteous quote out of them.'

'Makes good headlines, though.'

'And they shouldn't.'

'Now who's being self-righteous? You know what they called you in our office when you were running your *Stop the Rot* campaign? Miss Eyemright.'

'I am right, however. I'm right about that. And I certainly was about *Stop the Rot*.'

'Okay. You could've been about *Stop the Rot*. I'm not denying it. Even though you never made as much use of the *Star* as you might have done. You know, the media could have been very helpful to you. Don't misunderstand me. I don't mean just puffing you up into some sort of personality.'

'Oh, but I haven't misunderstood you. Papers like yours like to make a big thing of how they help bring criminals to justice. But I know the truth of it. You're into that because leaks from the police are what sell. So you won't get anything from me, not about why Dr Scholl's left the team, about his opposition to me issuing a challenge to—' She stopped herself. Or seemed to. 'Not about any damn thing, unless it's my considered judgement that the public need to know it.'

'Oh, well,' Tim Patterson said, with obvious haste, 'if that's your view of us, I can see there's no point in saying anything more.'

He scuttled away in the direction of King Street and the *Evening Star* office.

Harriet smiled again.

Once more toothy Marjorie came bursting into her room with the *Evening Star* flapping between her outspread hands like a demented cook's apron.

'Have you seen this? Have you seen this?'

Harriet looked up.

'If you're referring to that copy of the *Evening Star*, which you seem yet again to have reduced to an utter mess, you can hardly expect me to have seen it, since the early edition's presumably only just out and I've been here in my room this last hour and more.'

'Yes. Yes. I'm sorry. But, I mean, is it true? They've put your picture in again.'

'Until I see the wretched paper I can hardly tell you whether it's true or not. Or even what it is.'

'But look.' She managed to get the paper down on the desk, and with the front page uppermost. 'Look.'

Harriet looked down at the big black headline, with

her photograph in uniform under it, covering almost a quarter of the page.

TOP COP'S CHALLENGE TO COP KILLER

She had hardly flicked through the short, adjective-spangled story under Tim Patterson's by-line – he had, she conceded, in the minimal time she had allowed him made all that could be made of her single half-hint – before her direct line phone buzzed. Like an angry wasp.

She picked it up.

'Sir Michael? I think I can guess what you're calling about.'

'Well, is there any truth in what that infernal young man says?'

'No, sir. I know issuing a challenge to Grace Brown was an idea I proposed to you some time ago, when I think Dr Scholl more or less gave it his backing or at least said it might be an answer. But you rejected it, and on second thoughts I agreed that there was more of the stunt about the idea than of the justified manoeuvre. So I did, and said, no more about it.'

'I'm glad to hear it. But then how did that young man get hold of the notion? It wasn't Scholl, surely.'

'No, sir. I think one can discount that altogether. As I said, his backing for the idea was at best half-hearted. There were too many incalculables about it, he said. And he has a reputation to maintain. He wouldn't go gossiping to the press.'

'Which leaves it all a mystery. And one I'd like to see cleared up.'

'Well, sir, I've just been thinking. And I can guess perhaps what may have happened. It could have been that the young man, Patterson, simply misunderstood some passing reference.'

She hurried on.

'But the main point is, sir, what the next step should be. I mean, once something like this has been put into the public domain, it's going to be very difficult to withdraw it without it looking like weakness on our part. A sudden attack of cowardice even . . .'

There was a silence at the other end of the line.

A thought tickled Harriet's mind: the sound of a Chief Constable thinking.

'Yes. Yes, I see what you mean. But we can't let ourselves be led by the nose by a tuppeny-ha'penny rag like the *Evening Star*. Surely we can simply deny the story.'

'Well, I've a feeling the general public would hardly believe us. You know how the average person thinks what they see in print is the truth, and thousands of people in the city will have read in the *Evening Star* that a challenge has been issued. They won't take into account the lack of detail. All those screaming adjectives will have blotted that out, as our Mr Patterson intended. And then, sir, there's another factor. Tomorrow morning the whole of the national press will be repeating the story. Which will have been on TV, and certainly on the Birchester radios, all evening.'

'But can't we issue a notice of some sort . . . A request to editors? They've co-operated in that way in the past.'

'Well, yes, sir. But that's only been in things like kidnapping cases where it was important not to let the kidnappers know the police had been informed.'

'Yes. Yes, I suppose so. So what you're saying, Miss Martens, is what's done is done. That it?'

'Yes, sir. I think really it is.'

'So there now comes the question of how we're going to let this situation develop.'

'Or rather, how we're going to make it develop, sir.'

'Make it develop? You see some advantages in it all, then?'

'Well, I do, sir. We've been reacting, so far, to whatever that madwoman's seen fit to try. Really we've just only been taking precautions. Quite rightly, of course. I'd quit the Service if I thought anything I'd omitted to do had brought about the death of a fellow officer. But beyond searching for Grace Brown – and, with so little o go on, that was always going to be a needle-in-a-haystack business – we've been unable to make the running ourselves. And it's only when you're doing that you force the enemy into making wrong moves. *Stop the Rot* proved that, I think. Or was proving it.'

'Yes. You certainly made your point there. And your idea is that we should adopt the same tactics here?'

'Yes, sir, it is. If at tomorrow's press conference I confirm the reports in the papers – and there'll be plenty to confirm, I'm sure – then I can use plain words to get at that woman. I'd be almost willing to bet that's what'll bring her out into our sights. And if what I say then doesn't do it, I'll use plainer and plainer words until it does.'

'Well, it's a hard course to take, Miss Martens. Damn hard.'

'Let's say I'm a hard detective, sir.'

Chapter Fourteen

In Harriet's call from Sir Michael – not ended until she had agreed that Dr Scholl should be asked urgently to return – she had forecast altogether correctly the effect of that hastily pieced together story in the *Evening Star*, short of hard facts though it was.

That evening the television news programmes put out guarded versions of it, going little further than hinting at revelations to come, the BBC draining any too vivid impact in a froth of abstract words, ITN putting over the story with its implications all too plain but just out of sight, Sky TV blatant. But it was in the morning that the national press, led by the populars in full inventive cry, made what had under Tim Patterson's by-line been only a cleverly plumped-up piece of gossip into something that readers up and down the land would take for gospel.

The power of the press. In Harriet's head a dose of sharp contempt mingled with a tiny jet of pleasure in a scheme well executed.

It now remained only to underline for the busily scribbling reporters at her press conference, and to show the little red eyes of the TV cameras, that what had until now been so much guesswork was the reality. Top Cop was challenging Cop Killer.

Nicely convenient that the first frantically raised hand at the conference should be one she recognized as coming from a popular paper with some pretensions to seriousness.

'It's the *Herald*, isn't it?'

'Superintendent, there have been reports that you have issued a personal challenge to the woman the police believe has killed five police officers. Are they correct?'

'Yes, I can give you a straight answer to that. I am challenging Grace Brown, the woman who's been labelled Cop Killer. I'm challenging her to meet me head to head.'

A gratifying intake of breath distinctly audible from among the crammed media hounds. Microphones thrust even more eagerly forward, notebook pages flipped over and over as if that mere action somehow ratified what had been said.

'When you say *head to head* what exactly is it you have in mind, Superintendent?'

'Just this. If Grace Brown is intent on killing yet another police officer, let her come out and find me. I won't be hiding away. I promise you that.'

God knows what Sir Michael's going to make of this. But he gave the go-ahead, and if he hasn't had the nous to work out the implications, too bad for him. Bringing Dr Smellyfeet back is hardly going to make everything safe and comfortable.

'Does that mean, Superintendent, you'll be walking the streets of Birchester, letting her get at you?'

And, before she had time to answer, another question shouted up.

'Superintendent, am I right in thinking that if Cop Killer's following that list in – whatsit, the Book of Ecstas— Book of Exodus – she'll be intending to inflict a *wound for wound*?'

'I imagine she will.'

'But, Superintendent, will that be just a wound? Or will she, as she has up to now, be aiming to kill whoever she's wounding?'

'I imagine she will.'

'And, Superintendent, you'll be out on the street waiting for her to try and inflict some fatal wound on you?'

'I've said as much, yes.'

'Will you have protection, Superintendent?'

'What would you feel if I'd answered that question fully and, thanks to what you'd printed, Grace Brown was able to commit a seventh murder on some other unsuspecting police officer and get away with it?'

Dr Smellyfeet, looming, pinker of face than ever, was waiting for her in her office when, at last, the hounds at the conference had ceased going round and round repeating versions of questions already answered.

'Harriet, what the hell have you done?'

'Taken your advice perhaps, Peter?'

'No.'

The little pink patch of baldness nestling among his abundant dark curls – Harriet could see it as he leant

forward and in his fury slapped her desk, double-
handed – went even pinker.

'No, no, I never advised you to do anything as
absolutely crazy as this.'

'I think you did. If not without a good ration of
face-saving get-outs. You did, you know, actually say to
me – it was just before I first read your Profile – that a
direct challenge to Grace might bring her to the light of
day. You see I've said *might*. It was the word you actually used. So you won't have too much on your
conscience.'

'Very sharp. But, I seem to remember, when we had
that conversation I told you Sir Michael would never
agree to such a— Was *stunt* the word I used?'

'It was. I used it myself to him when he agreed
that we could do nothing other than go ahead after the
Evening Star had produced their story.'

'And it was you told them? Before you'd got any
agreement from your Chief Constable?'

'Yes, you're right to sound surprised. I'd be surprised myself, I'd have been astonished, if that had
been the way it happened.'

Dr Scholl gave her a quick look.

'Then, Harriet, how did it happen? How did that
fellow Peterson, Parkinson, Patterson, get hold of even
a glimmer of an idea of this sort?'

'That would be telling.'

'And you're not going to tell?'

'Perhaps there's nothing to tell. But whether there is
or there isn't, you're not going to hear.'

'Not even if I think it's relevant to the advice which
Sir Michael, who to tell the truth seemed to be in

something of a panic, asked me to give you when he phoned last night?'

'And what advice would that be?'

'If I had my way, it would be to go on TV tonight and say that, at the urging of the well-known forensic psychologist, Dr Peter Scholl, you have decided not to pursue your challenge.'

'Ha, ha.'

'Yes. Well, I didn't expect you'd listen. After all, you're the one who believes she's always right.'

'Back to that, are we? Nevertheless, I still think I am right to be doing this. Okay, I know that I'm not equipped to see into the mind of a madwoman like Grace Brown, and I don't really know what this will do to her. But I do know that I can't ultimately lose. If it does bring her out from her hole before she acts on whatever plan she has to kill one of the Greater Birchester Force in some *wound for wound* manner – and I had some confirmation yesterday from her ex-husband in Australia, whom we've at last managed to contact, that she always was a planner – then I've won. If it doesn't, then at least I've acted. I've tried.'

'Oh, yes, you may succeed in bringing her out from wherever she's hiding. But it's all too likely that it'll be at the cost of the member of your Force she kills being Detective Superintendent Harriet Martens.'

'All right, at that cost. But, remember, this is relying on your advice.' She tapped with a crooked forefinger on the blue cover of the Profile, as ever on her desk. 'Grace, the planner, will have long ago thought out how she can bring off a *wound for wound* murder. But now with a new target and challenged to act immediately she'll have to improvise, and there she may come unstuck as she could have done when she hastily went for Froggy Froggott. So, though, yes, I'm offering myself as a sacrificial goat, if you like, I'm not such a fool as to do it out of any sort of damn silly bravado. I told Sir Michael last night that I was a hard detective, and this is what being hard means. It doesn't mean simply being stupid.'

Harriet had refused to give Dr Smellyfeet precise details of how she actually intended to make good her challenge. She was too aware that, if he or anyone in the Force knew exactly what she proposed, they would almost certainly mount some kind of surveillance on her. And she had too much respect for Grace not to believe that, cunning as she was, she would detect the presence of police shadowers however skilful.

In her head she recited the litany of her enemy's successes of the past. And of the future, if she was not stopped now.

Life for life
Eye for eye
Tooth for tooth
Hand for hand
Foot for foot
Burning for burning
Wound for wound
Stripe for stripe

She knew – she, too, could make plans – just where it

was that she was going out to meet with Grace. If Grace was going to respond . . . If, hiding as the Profile had forecast somewhere within a cut-off radius centred on the Queen Street police station, she had been able to get hold of the *Evening Star*, if she had heard Greater Birchester Radio . . . If in fact she had actually been goaded into changing whatever plan she had made to attack some other police officer *wound for wound*.

The chosen site was the towpath of the Birchester–Liverpool Canal.

There was, Harriet had reasoned, really only one place inside Dr Smellyfeet's circle where Grace could count on meeting her without any other person present: the section of the canal that ran through the area of Greater Birchester Police B Division. It had for long been largely derelict. The huge warehouses, which had once loaded their goods on to barges to chug their way, or be pulled by lumbering horses, to Liverpool and the markets of the world, were almost all empty, patched with estate agents' boards grown all but illegible from years of beating rain and months of scanty summer sun. The rolls of barbed wire on the tops of the high brick walls of the mills, put there for the short time the buildings were expected to be vacant so as to keep out intruders with an eye on movable objects, had long ago been rusted into near extinction. Even the occasional graffiti of later years – *Up the Rovers* on the far side walls, *United Rule* on the Queen Street area side – had faded almost to nothing.

The towpaths on either bank did provide short cuts between areas of the city, but few people seemed to need nowadays to make those journeys. In the early mornings and at the evening rush-hour a few hunched men on bicycles would skim along the gritty black paths swerving round the places where scrawny bushes had established a hold in the sour earth below. But otherwise the towpaths were almost entirely deserted. Boys sometimes attempted to fish from them, though the canal's sullen greeny-grey water smelling faintly of things chemical was hardly encouraging. Only the really desperate love-makers occasionally risked the dank and unlovely stretches on either bank.

Altogether the best and likeliest tilting-ground for an encounter. Perhaps a life-and-death encounter.

At 3 p.m. Harriet, after having gone home and changed from her customary dark-grey suit into uniform – How else will Grace know who I am? – began her vigil, pacing the gritty towpath of the bank on the inside of Dr Smellyfeet's cut-off circle, with the sharp spring breeze reddening her cheeks as she strode into it. She carried no gun, despite being entitled to do so and despite Grace Brown still possessing, presumably, the knife she had used to kill PC Titmuss. But she scarcely thought that joining combat with as elderly a woman required a firearm. However, she had put into the pocket of her uniform jacket a set of brass knuckles, a souvenir kept somewhat illegally and sentimentally from the first arrest she had ever made.

Grace Brown, the woman who had succeeded in killing five police officers and one ex-policeman, was not an adversary to be taken altogether lightly. Yet Harriet, fit and with her early training in self-defence and arrest techniques by no means forgotten, felt confident in taking the risk of doing without the back-up that might all too easily alert Grace, the cunning wild animal.

Otherwise she had in her shoulder-bag, its flap unfastened, the mobile phone no senior officer on duty could be without.

It squeaked now.

Harriet looked up and down the bleak length of the canal before she took out the phone. No one in sight.

'Superintendent Martens here.'

'Harriet, it's Peter Scholl. Where are you?'

'You know damn well where I am. I'm somewhere inside the Scholl Profile circle, waiting to meet somebody.'

'Oh, well, I just hoped I might trick you into telling the truth. I'm pretty anxious about you as a matter of fact.'

'I dare say. But much as I appreciate your concern you're not exactly helping me to look as if I'm a defenceless target. Which is the object of the exercise.'

'But, Harriet—'

Phone aerial rammed hard down.

Relentless march resumed. All the way along beside the lightly stinking water, ruffled from time to time, when the wind gusted, into looking like a miniature sea. To the far end of the Profile's flat-topped circle. Then on for a hundred yards or so beyond, to halt in the deep shadow beneath a bridge that had once linked two mills on either bank of the canal, a tunnel of blank sheets of rusty corrugated iron.

Further along came the Chapeltown area where in days gone by streets of labourers' housing had clustered round a single large, resolutely impressive Nonconformist chapel. Batley Street, where Grace Brown had set her fire trap, lay at the far end of it, and Harriet suspected she was still hiding somewhere among the rows of little back-to-back houses, as many empty and falling to pieces as occupied. But so far none of the search parties she had had sent out each day had found even the least clue to her lair. It was the nearness of the area to the most deserted stretch of the canal that had finally made her choose this as the place for an encounter.

Wait four or five minutes under the blind bridge, looking with apparent carelessness this way and that. Resume march in opposite direction.

Fifteen minutes' slow walk, eyes from time to time flicking towards the gaps between the huge looming warehouses or to the rusty doors that had once given access to the towpath. Then she had reached the far end of the line which the canal formed flattening Dr Smellyfeet's circle based on Queen Street police station. Further along, towards the municipal calm of Waterloo Gardens, lay the area where the towpaths on either side achieved a semblance of life. The City Council had decreed a canalside walk here and placed benches at intervals, neat wastebins decorated with the City arms beside them. Narrow lawns had been created behind the paths, dotted now with the rain-battered, yet still more or less colourful, remains of late purple and white crocuses. Here disused warehouses had been turned into blocks of smart flats, even though the view from them was still of semi-stagnant greenish water.

No longer likely territory for the skulking, gaunt presence of Grace Brown, who, if Dr Smellyfeet had got it right, would for this encounter be wearing her shapeless blue woolly hat.

Soon dusk added shades of dull grey to the warehouse walls as Harriet marched to and fro between the Walk and the blind bridge. Harder now to see if a figure was lurking in the narrow gaps between the towering dilapidated buildings. In a few minutes, no doubt, a handful of cyclists would come whirring rapidly along towards tea and television, creating an interval when no sudden attack was likely. And then . . . in the fully gathered dusk?

Harriet extracted a small torch from her pocket, ready to direct its light to the ground at her feet and to reflect upwards enough to show the person using it was wearing a skirt in regulation police blue. When it was altogether dark would a tall, gaunt woman come running out from one of the yet darker gaps, eight-inch-long kitchen knife raised to strike? *Wound for wound?*

A rat scuttled across the path and she decided to switch on the torch. Head moving from side to side, if less theatrically than before, eyes kept away from the reflected glare, she strode on, peering in the now almost complete darkness towards the least sound – a drip-drip-dripping from some broken pipe – the faintest glimpse of movement.

She was within a hundred yards of the blind bridge once more, and wondering whether it might be sensible to end her vigil there for this first trial, when, piercing the cold silence, her mobile beeped.

Aerial up.

'Yes?'

'Superintendent Martens, ma'am?'

'Yes? What is it?' A mouth-tight mutter in the night air.

'Ma'am, another murder.'

Chapter Fifteen

Grace Brown, it turned out, had not committed her seventh murder. But she had severely wounded an officer on point-duty. Police Constable Venning had been stabbed in the side of the neck – much as PC Titmuss had been at the start of the series of killings – as he stood on his own, in accordance with the modification of the order for officers in uniform to be paired. He had been directing traffic at the point where it infiltrated from Market Place into Queen Street, barely two hundred yards from the police station. The very place – the thought had at once entered Harriet's head – where WPC Syed had been blinded, *eye for eye*.

When she reached the scene there was little indication that anything had happened. PC Venning had been rushed to hospital and his place taken by another officer, looking more than a little apprehensive as he directed the traffic jostling past again at the fag-end of the rush-hour. Almost the only signs of the attack were the uniformed officers going about among the hurrying crowds attempting in the early dark to find witnesses. DI Johnston, the inspector from her team who had got to the scene first, explained that apparently Grace had darted across to where PC Venning stood, stabbed him, and then had darted as quickly to the far side. Only when Venning was seen lying in the roadway had people become aware of something having happened.

While Harriet was still getting the facts one of the officers drafted in to look for witnesses, Sergeant Grant, from the Queen Street rape unit, brought up a twenty-year-old girl, her face blotched with tear stains.

'Evening, ma'am. I think you'll want to hear what this young woman has to say. She may be about the only good witness left to us. She's been in shock since it happened, but I think she'll give you a decent account now.'

With a little murmuring encouragement from Sergeant Grant, the girl at last brought herself to speak.

'She come rushing just past me, biffed me elbow. That was— That's why I sort of took particular notice. We'd been waiting to cross, a whole lot of us. I was at the back and I thought I'd missed me chance, with the traffic revving up to move off again. And then, there came that sort of rushing from behind me, this tall old woman in – what? – one of them donkey jacket things with a kind of blue-like hat on her head. I dunno, but I had a feeling she'd been standing in the doorway of Boots the Chemist just behind where I was. They'd been closed about ten minutes. I know because I'd wanted to – Well, needed to— To buy some you-know-what's— sannies.'

'Take a deep breath and begin again,' Harriet said sharply.

'Yes. Yes, sorry, officer. But I—'

'This woman came rushing out from the doorway of Boots, and what happened?'

'She went rushing past me. And – the cars there were just moving off – she was half across the road before you could say Jack Rob— I mean, in just sort of half a second. And then I saw she had this knife in her hand. A sort of— Well, just a kitchen knife really. But a big one, the kind you use for cutting up meat for a stew. Well, my mum does.'

'Right,' Harriet bit in, 'she had a large kitchen knife. In which hand?'

'Which hand? I don't— Yes, in her left. Yes, the left.'

'Go on.'

'And then— Then— Oh, God, it was just awful.'

'Tell me exactly what it was she did. It's important. It's going to help us find her.'

The force of the words made the girl bring herself to a calmer state.

'Yes. Yes, I'll try. She— Well, that was all really. She just raised up that knife and went for him, the copper there directing traffic. She sort of jabbed it at him, the knife. In his neck. In the side, sort of, of his neck. Well, more than jabbed. She was strong. Strong. Was it the one the papers call Cop Killer?'

'I dare say it was.'

And wearing once again, almost certainly, the donkey jacket she had put on when she hid at the back of the dead-end passageway in New Street and darted forwards to kill PC Titmuss, illicit cigarette between his lips. As well as the blue hat which, according to Dr Smellyfeet, Grace Brown wore only when she was intent on revenge for her supposed injuries.

'And after she stabbed the constable in the road there what happened?'

'I dunno. I mean, I was—'

'Yes, you do know. You were there. You saw that woman stab the constable. You must have seen what happened after that.'

The girl stood there in front of Harriet, suddenly struck into rebellious silence.

'Come on, what happened next?'

'Please. Please. No. Well, yes. Yes, she pulled out the knife. There was blood on it. I could see the blood on it in the street lights half across the road from where I was standing. I'll never forget it. Never. She didn't wipe it nor nothing. She just sort of put her head down, run across to the far side and— And then sort of just walked away.'

'Where was she going? Which direction?'

'Oh God, I don't know. Leave me alone, can't you?'

'No. If we're going to find her we must know where she was heading for. Think. Remember. Tell me what you saw.'

'Yes. Yes, she went back along Queen Street. I remember now, I was sort of surprised. I thought she'd of gone the other way. But, no. She went back along Queen Street. I saw her - she's tall, you know, tallish anyhow - I saw her sort of blue hat, woolly, bobbing past the people coming down the street towards her. I don't think they'd even realized— I mean, how could they know what had happened? It was all so quick.'

'And that was the last you saw of her? Her blue hat bobbing along up Queen Street? In the direction of the police station, yes?'

'Yes, towards there. She wasn't going to give herself up, was she? I mean, if she's mad she might of . . .'

'No, I don't think she was going to give herself up.'

'Can I go home now? I— I'm feeling sort of sick.'

'Yes, all right, go. But give the sergeant your name and address.'

'Yes, yes. I will. Yes.'

The girl turned away, free from the clutches of the demanding figure she had been put in front of. And showing her relief even as Sergeant Grant led her away.

'You heard all that?' Harriet turned to DI Johnston.

'Aye, ma'am, I did, the silly wee creature.'

'Silly she may be, DI. But she's told us something we may be grateful for yet. If Grace Brown wasn't heading for the nick to beg to be arrested, where was she going? Why did she make off in that direction? The girl was perfectly right. You'd have expected her to go the other way, where the pavement's wider and the crowds begin to thin out.'

'Aye, I suppose so,' the DI said. 'And, true enough, there's Turner's Alley just there. Running between Queen Street and—'

'And Lime Street.'

Harriet tugged out her mobile, streamed out orders.

Lime Street. Leading almost straight down to the canal. The road where the carts used to bring up the limes from the Liverpool barges, directly from the West Indies. And just off to the left at the far end, Chapeltown. Row upon row of half-ruined labourers' houses. Somewhere there a place where Grace has been hiding.

And we're going to find it. And her. Before the day's out.

It might, just might, be possible to get enough

officers there in time to catch Grace. Out in the open before she manages to wriggle back into whatever hiding-place she has.

In time, she thought. But will we be in time? In time to stop Number Eight. *Stripe for stripe.*

She had been tempted to drive urgently down to Chapeltown herself. But a moment's thought, and she had known her first duty was to be in her office co-ordinating. This was the best chance of capturing the woman working her way through that grim Exodus list since the moment they had discovered she had been a worker in the Queen Street police canteen and had raided her room in that dingy house in Sullivan Street, only to find she had left hardly a quarter of an hour earlier. And for the trail, then, to peter out in blank failure. No gung-ho rushing about must spoil the chance now. So she sat at her desk, grabbing her phone at each incoming report, shooting out new orders in response. And hoping.

But would it be the same check again? A lair found, and no one in it?

Not unlikely. Grace, the planner, must have been prepared for an immediate police reaction to the lightning attack on the point-duty officer she had plotted. Perhaps she had calculated that, by getting away after it not in the obvious direction, she would be able to reach safety. And, except for the chance of that one witness being so shocked she had stayed there paralysed and seen, without seeing, that shapeless blue hat bobbing away, Grace might have disappeared cleanly as if she had been banished by a stage conjuror. As she might vanish yet.

Then, as the minutes went by without a sighting, a new thought seated itself in Harriet's head. Grace Brown was every bit as much of a challenger as herself. An avenger wanting the world to know she was killing police officers because she believed, at the obscure beginnings of it all in a mini-riot at an anti-abortion protest, the life of her unborn, last-hope child had been taken by the action of a police officer.

Then why – another thought presented itself – why had Grace not accepted the challenge that had screamed at her from the front-page headline of the *Evening Star*, from the excited voices of radio reporters? Why, this afternoon at the stretch of canal so near Chapeltown instead of darting her lightning attack on PC Venning, had she not come out there, with that kitchen knife? Why from somewhere between two of the great tall dilapidated buildings on the towpath had she not leapt with knife upraised? Why as dusk had fallen and there was only the occasional sigh of a gust of wind, the scuttle of a rat, the sudden inexplicable dripping from some broken pipe, had Grace not come, shapeless blue hat on head, for that confrontation?

Had she perhaps, fixed in her long resolve, simply dismissed the notion of meeting head to head the woman leading the hunt for her? Were the planner's plans so set in stone that nothing would alter them?

If so, had all the contrivance of getting that challenge issued gone for nothing? Had the risk willingly taken, but not without counting the possible cost, been not in any way worthwhile? Had the real possibility of disciplinary disaster, no less, if that gamble had gone awry, proved to have been to no purpose?

And, worse, when the passing minutes had turned to hours and the phone calls obstinately repeated nil results, the thought grew sharper and heavier: was there now no way of preventing Grace reaching to the end of her long catalogue of death? If she had in her fixed determination been able to ignore the challenge thrown down to her, was there any way, except to hope for some lucky chance, of preventing the death of yet another Greater Birchester Police officer?

She looked at her watch. Midnight would be the time to sign off hope. Half an hour to go.

And then her mobile sounded, and DI Johnston's voice crackled in her ear, dourly keeping down the excitement he was plainly feeling.

'We've found her place, ma'am. One of the patrols— I was just about to call them off, and then—'

'Grace Brown? You've got her?'

'No, ma'am. No, the bird had flown, as they say. But—'

'How long before? Any sign which way she went?'

'No, ma'am, she must have left right after stabbing PC Venning, from the look of it. But she can't have gone far, even if she has succeeded in hiding herself away again. With all the uniforms I've had going up and down the streets, she'd have been bound to be spotted if she'd tried to get right away.'

'Inspector, I'm coming down. Where are you?'

*

It was not even inside a house. DI Johnston, a little miffed at having his triumph abruptly set aside, had been waiting for her at the doorless doorway of an almost totally derelict narrow, two-storey dwelling – 'Bulldozers in next month,' he had muttered – and had led her through to a shed in the tiny yard behind, the beam of his torch pointing to a missing floorboard here and there as they went.

The shed, still in a reasonable state of repair, door intact, an open padlock hanging from the hasp, took up almost a third of the space of the yard. Inside it, DI Johnston's slowly moving torch beam revealed little beside an old mattress on the floor against one of the shrivelled wooden walls with a rucked-up grey blanket on it. And, yes, surely, too, an old royal-blue donkey jacket.

'Shine your torch on that jacket, DI.'

'Ma'am.'

In the strong beam of the torch, held close, it was easy to see on the greasy cloth a dark stain that could well be old dried blood.

'Yes. Get this to Forensic and they'll find it's Titmuss's blood on it. Bound to be. So we'll have some evidence – if we ever get the woman to court.'

Over the shed's one grimy window another piece of blanket had been draped, although the chance of the light inside being seen must have been absurdly remote. The planner planning for every last contingency, even the absolutely minimal risk from the gleam of the stub of a candle fastened by its melted wax to the floor. Beside that there lay a tin plate with, still there as evidence of recent occupation, half a crust of a sliced loaf. In the far corner some scraps of paper, including the wrapper from the loaf, were the only other indications that it had been here that Grace had evaded all the police searchers' efforts.

'You've looked through that pile?' Harriet asked.

'I have, ma'am. Turned it over myself. It'll be bagged for Forensic in just a minute. May be a print or two on something, for what it's worth. But otherwise nothing of any significance.'

'Could you tell where she'd been buying her bread?'

'No, ma'am. Everything only what you might get at any little corner shop.'

'All right. So, what about that?'

Harriet pointed to an object on the floor half-hidden by the shed door. A battered little plastic transistor lying on its back, made almost invisible by engrained dust.

'Yes, I did see that, ma'am. But it's plain it was thrown down there long before the former occupants left. Three, four, five years ago. Judging by the look of it.'

'Does it work?'

'Work? I shouldna' think it was working even five years ago.'

Harriet picked up the dusty, cracked object with her gloved hands and flicked at the volume switch. It had been in the 'on' position, but when she clicked it to and fro a tiny crackling could be heard. But no more.

She turned the little box round and, with one probing finger, peeled away the damp-soft, hole-punched cardboard sheet on the back.

'Shine your torch in,' she said to the DI.

185

By its light she was able to see the pair of dry cells that had powered the thing.

'Yes. Batteries not five years old, not by any means. But I rather think these must be exhausted. Step outside, and we'll try them in your torch if they fit.'

The DI had caught on by now.

'You're saying she's been toting that old radio round with her, ma'am? And left it here just because it'd gone kaput? She's been keeping in touch with police activities that way?'

'Thanks in the first place to our friends in the media. Ever helpful.'

A little fumbling in the faint light from a cloud-covered moon and it was confirmed that the transistor had been run until its batteries were all but dead.

'And that accounts, DI,' Harriet said, unusually communicative in the pleasure of her discovery, 'for Grace Brown seeming to decline the challenge blared out at her on radio, on TV, in the *Evening Star*. You realize there was no newspaper among that pile in the corner in there?'

'Yes, of course, ma'am. So, do you think she'd have had a go at you somewhere, if she'd known?'

'Let's say I'm pretty sure of it.'

At home at last, in her silent, empty house, she resolutely put into practice her system of sleep-going. Relax the body, feet, legs, small of back, chest, arms, hands, neck, facial muscles. Close eyes. Wait for the sudden paradoxical chips of vision from the subconscious. Turn over. Oblivion.

Chapter Sixteen

Out of the short night's oblivion one glimmer of hope manifested itself as a waking thought. Might there be a way, even now, of putting that challenge before the madwoman still intent on murder? Even if Grace had had to abandon the dust-dark plastic radio which had helped her to out-plot the best efforts of Greater Birchester Police? Even if, perhaps, she no longer risked going out to buy an *Evening Star*, like the one left in the Sullivan Street house? If that challenge was plastered on newspaper bills all over Chapeltown's grimy, now rain-soaked streets, could it reach her even at this late moment?

Top Cop's Challenge – Cop Killer Challenge – Top Cop Seeks Meeting – Killer or Cop Who Will Win?

Harriet imagined them.

Would bills like that take the situation back to where it had been twenty-four hours earlier? By the end of the day now would a second solitary march up and down the deserted stretch of the canal bring about the sudden onrush from the shadows she had expected before? Or would it need another day before it came? Two more days? A week of unwatched pacing that length of towpath?

But perhaps the pairs of officers she intended to have go through Chapeltown today, rain or shine, poking into every such empty house as the one where DI Johnston had found Grace's latest lair would, even in two or three hours' time, have brought the hunt to a whirl-of-action conclusion.

Still, before leaving home she made a telephone call.

'Queen Street police station. CID Room.'

'Superintendent Martens here. Who's on duty now?'

'Oh, good morning, ma'am. Or rather, rotten rainy morning. DC Sparks here.'

For an instant the recollection of Froggy Froggott's *I don't want a weather report: I want action* came back to her.

But what she wanted now was co-operation.

'And who else is with you?'

'Well, ma'am, there's only just the two of us here this early, me and DC Brewer.'

'Right. Good, good. I'll have a word with Brewer.'

Brewer was one of those detectives who never aspire to rise higher than the lowest rank in the CID. But, once he had been transferred into plain clothes, he had been in his element. Sources of information collected up and down the B Division area, a list of informers the envy of any detective of any rank, friends and acquaintances everywhere, and a few enemies. A happy record of arrests, even if almost all for the lesser crimes.

Bill. Yes, that was his name.

'Bill, good morning.'

'Ma'am?'

A touch of caution. Unused to hard-woman Detective Chief Inspector Martens – as she had been when he had come directly under her – unbending to this extent.

'Tell me, do you happen to know anybody in the *Evening Star* printing works?'

'I wouldn't be surprised if I did, ma'am. Print workers are generally pretty fond of a pint.'

'Good. So let me, when I can, buy a drink for you and any friend of yours there, if you can bring one to mind.'

'I never say no to an offer like that, ma'am. Or not unless I think I'm being asked to step too far out of line.'

'Ah, no. Nothing of that sort. It's just that there is something I want doing. Without those nosy bastards of *Evening Star* reporters reading anything into it.'

'Then I dare say I could help you, ma'am.'

Before she had to stand in front of yet another press conference, Harriet, wearing uniform in anticipation of an encounter at the day's end on the bank of the deserted canal, took one more step in her struggle with Grace Brown. *Wound for wound* had been reached in Grace's Exodus tariff. Reached and paid for. But one more bloody exhortation remained: *stripe for stripe*. How was Grace to be thwarted, if somehow she failed to see the renewed newspaper bill challenge DC Bill Brewer should be quietly getting organized? Or if, in her one-track determination, she ignored it?

What plan now must the plan-maker be making? There was one obvious obstacle Grace would have to overcome. *Stripe for stripe* plainly implied a Greater Birchester Police officer being somehow flogged and then killed. One of the reporters from the nationals had even, at the conference after the death of PC Strachan, taken the opportunity to ask a lip-smacking question about the hunt for Grace Brown not being over before a woman police officer was whipped. But if Grace was going to attempt something of this sort, and after her killing *hand for hand* of Cadet Chatterton and her yet more perversely ingenious murder *foot for foot* of ex-PC Studley no one could doubt she could do it, she must first of all get hold of the necessary implement. And, thanks to the way she had been successfully harried, she almost certainly no longer had access to anywhere that, well in advance, she might have hidden a whip. So it was altogether likely now that she would have to attempt to get hold of one. And, in late twentieth-century Birchester, whips were no longer everyday purchasable items. In fact, probably the only place to get one would be at a sex shop.

So, at her briefing she tasked half a dozen members of her team with visiting every sex shop in Birchester – they were mostly to be found in the city's sleazy quarter, Moorfields – to get the staff, warned not to attempt to detain this unlikely but dangerous customer, to report at once any purchase by an elderly woman of any sort of whip. At the last moment, too, against all her feelings about letting no infringement of the law however minor go untouched, Harriet added a rider. Some indication could be given that co-operation would be rewarded with less police attention.

Then off to meet the press, the red-eyed TV

cameras, the waving stubby microphones. With the secret comfort of thinking that, probably before it was over, thanks to Detective Constable Brewer, newspaper bill after newspaper bill would be on their way through the city's rain-slicked streets to Chapeltown to be pasted on blank walls – plenty of those down there – or stuck up in front of all the remaining little shops still open among the black-windowed, deserted houses.

'Superintendent, can you tell us what precautions were in place when PC Gary Venning was stabbed while on point-duty, alone, in Queen Street last evening?'

It was Tim Patterson, once again.

'The normal precautions when there is a repeat murderer uncaught.'

'Can you tell us what those precautions were?'

'Certainly not. The woman who attacked PC Venning is still at large.'

'Then can you say what attempts were made to apprehend her last night?'

'Yes. Thanks to diligent work under Detective Inspector Johnston the place where we suspect the attacker was living was discovered.'

A gratifying murmur of interest. Something reflecting credit on Greater Birchester Police at last going to appear in the papers?

'But no clues were found there that got you anywhere?'

Tim Patterson well informed as usual. One day his source will be worth discovering. And punishing. But, no, there won't be any words of praise for good police-work now.

'If we have found helpful evidence it naturally will have to be kept confidential.'

Another reporter bobbing up. And about time. One of the nationals by the look of her.

'Superintendent, I understand that an order for Birchester Police officers in uniform not to go about on their own was rescinded, and then put back in place. Can you explain how it came about, then, that Police Constable Venning was exposed to an attack that might well have been fatal, when he was entirely on his own?'

Yes, gabby enough to be a national paper reporter being given a try-out on us poor provincials. And easy enough to answer.

'PC Venning was hardly *entirely on his own*. He was on point-duty in what, at that hour of the evening, is perhaps the most crowded area in the whole of Birchester.'

Slap.

But, no. Tim Patterson up on his feet again. And practically shouting.

'Crowded the Queen Street area may be, Superintendent, but it wasn't exactly crowded with police officers when Cop Killer struck again. *Wound for wound* as the Good Book has it – and as you must surely have been expecting.'

'Is that a question, Mr Patterson? Or an extract from one of the *Evening Star* leaders?'

Mistake. Keep patient.

'Well, this is my question then: why was PC Venning left exposed like that?'

Mistake punished.

Harriet drew a breath.

'I'll tell you why. Policing is a matter of war. The police, the forces of law and order, are at war with the criminals in our midst. We are. We always have been. And I dare say we always will be. You, Mr Patterson, as a crime reporter, should be well aware of that. But perhaps you are not so aware of this. That in a war commanders have to give orders that endanger the lives of the men and women under them. They know they are endangering them. And they still have to give those orders. I knew that PC Venning, like all the other officers sent on point-duty on their own, was there at some risk, even some considerable risk. But it was a necessary risk. The city of Birchester cannot be policed by officers in pairs day after day, on and on, and everywhere. So I modified the order that any officer in uniform must go about with another. Point-duty was one of the exceptions I made. And I stand by that. Unhesitatingly.'

Late afternoon was the time Harriet had fixed on as being the earliest she could expect Grace Brown to go dodging through the dingy streets of Chapeltown to the deserted canal, still the likeliest place for her to respond to the challenge. If, in yet deeper hiding somewhere after her attack on PC Venning, she had even seen the newspaper bills. If she was not at this moment, blaring bills seen and ignored, simply slipping through the early rainy dusk to Moorfields, its porn bookstores, sex-trap clubs and garish sex-shops, a little hoard of money tucked somewhere among her nondescript clothes, nothing diverting her from her progress to a death *stripe for stripe.*

Just about to leave, giving Marjorie some more or less likely reason for her absence, there came a tentative tap on her half-open door and Rob Roberts appeared.

With, over his arm, the ancient gardening mac lent to him on another rainy Birchester day.

Ready to go out on a self-imposed task she knew to be risking her life, the sight of Rob holding out like an offering that almost forgotten coat, set up a simmering rage in her.

'Mrs Piddock, I've been meaning to bring you this for weeks, and then when I saw this morning the way it was raining, I thought I'd . . .' The excuse died away into feebleness.

Harriet might have let it go. After all, Rob Roberts was full of good intentions, if nothing else. But his use of her married name, especially in front of flapping-eared Marjorie, sent her anger shooting up to break-out point.

'Inspector, I think I told you on a previous occasion that I do not want my married name used in official circumstances. Are you accustomed to making a play with it? You assured me once that what was in your confidential files was confidential. Is that true?'

Rob Roberts' ruddy-skinned face darkened at once in a furious blush.

Harriet pounced.

'I can see it's not. So, tell me, do you go round showing off your chance bit of knowledge by calling me Mrs Piddock at every possible opportunity?'

'No. No, I never . . . Well, I must confess, I suppose just sometimes . . .'

'Just how many times? Just when and where?'

It was hardly fair, but Rob's weak piffling and paffling was testing her over-stretched nerves to breaking-point.

She stood waiting for his answer. He was going to get away with nothing.

'Well, ma'am, I wasn't exactly counting up.' But the tiny flare died away at once. 'I mean, I can remember talking about you in the Queen Street canteen once. It was when the newspapers had begun making a thing about you and *Stop the Rot*, and the lads were amused. Or, well, no, interested. They were just interested to know what your real name was. There was a bit of joking, I suppose. Someone said the papers would never have called you the Hard Detective if the name you'd used was Piddock. That raised a bit of a laugh, but I—I think that was almost all, really, ma'am.'

She checked her anger. Softy Rob Roberts was hardly worth wasting it on.

'Oh, very well. But don't do it again. And thanks for the coat. Just dump it on my chair, will you?'

She swung away, mind already intent on the rain-soaked towpath of the canal.

But at the canal – it was still raining, if more feebly: no one was about – she found she was still unsettled from the effect of that unexpected spat with Rob. Firmly pursing her lips, she made herself stop at the last bench of polite Canalside Walk, wet though it was. She swept off the excess rainwater with one hand, turned and sat, the brass knuckles that bulged her jacket pocket giving a muffled clunk as she did so. Then she fought to clear her mind.

Stupid to go to encounter a fixated madwoman unless she was in full possession of her faculties.

Five minutes did it.

She got up, brushed at the back of her damp skirt and set out at a steady pace for the blind bridge at the other end of her patrol. Taking care not to appear to be looking about her too sharply, she nevertheless gave a single quick glance into every dark nook where a would-be attacker might hide.

Would this be what Grace Brown would attempt? Simply a single vicious attack, suddenly leaping out at the woman she would in all likelihood have now seen described on dozens of newspaper bills as Top Cop. Or would Grace after all do no more than speak? Hurl words of abuse? Tell this representative of the hated police that she had had her revenge till almost the last dregs? And meant to go on till the cup was drained?

Already on this day of hovering rain clouds dusk seemed to be descending.

Chapter Seventeen

Under the louring rain clouds, seeping now only an off-and-on drizzle, Harriet went pacing the canal's black towpath, her feet squelching slightly on the gritty surface at every step. The walls of the long-deserted warehouses at her side glistened with so much damp that they seemed to be made as much of water as of brick. The sluggish green canal itself, its filmed-over surface lightly pocked with the descending droplets, was giving off a yet sharper odour, metallic and clinging.

She stared ahead, eyes smarting, though in the mistiness it was impossible to see very far. Nothing. Nobody. Not even any of the stray cats she had seen on her last visit. She turned to look to the side. The *For Sale* and *To Let* boards, still just visible, drooped above her, less legible than ever for their coating of rain. The graffiti, too, were robbed in this sodden atmosphere of such slapdash aggressiveness as they once must have had.

Carefully she set herself, as she strode cautiously onwards, to locate and note each possible place where a lurker might be hiding.

A patch at the top of a once eight-foot wall had crumbled away. Someone might be able to scramble up on the far side and launch themselves from that vantage point. But from the towpath there was no possibility of getting up high enough to see over.

A hundred yards further on a sheet of plasterboard that had blocked a tall upper window had rotted away. Could someone inside there leap down in one single move? Would they – would tall angular Grace Brown? – land nimbly enough to be able to . . . To do what? There was no telling, no telling at all.

Between two of the towering warehouses she saw a narrow gap, ignored the day before. It was only four, perhaps five inches wide, but that might, she thought, be enough for gaunt Grace Brown. She peered into the inner blackness between the two sides. But there was no more to see than the walls reaching up and up, blankly.

Another window, equally high up in the wall of its building, had been protected by iron bars, and it was just possible to see, craning upwards, that all three of the centre ones had rusted right away. So would Grace be able to force herself through that gap, drop down some old length of rope, lower herself unseen? To wait in the mist for her moment.

She turned away, trudged on. Squelch, squelch, squelch.

And now abruptly she began to doubt whether she had been justified in taking the course she had. More clearly than in the first flush of daring the day before she saw how easy it would be for a determined attacker to spring down on her . . . from nowhere, knife in hand. The knife which the girl at the kerb where PC Venning had been attacked had seen gleaming dark with blood.

Or, somehow, might Grace come flailing a whip, already bought and hidden somewhere and now brought out. Or, if a widespread, kite-like body was launched from one of the vantage points in the tall, foreboding buildings, striking with utter unexpectedness, it could well send a victim hurtling before they knew what was happening into the thick green waters of the canal. Even to drown there.

A rat, in the last of the rain-obscured daylight, came out from underneath a tangle of brambles a few yards further on, and went, intent on its own business, to the towpath edge. Harriet was unable to prevent herself kicking a stone hard in its direction.

Then, appalled by the loudness of the noise her unthinking action had set up, she stopped in her tracks. Had she given away her exact position to a pair of straining ears underneath a shapeless blue woollen hat?

She stood listening, her own ears at full stretch. But no alien sound followed. Nothing but the tiny whispering of the soft rain.

Onwards.

A grim rusty door, also neglected in her previous march. She put out a hand and pushed at it. Resistance. Then, just as she had told herself it was securely in place beyond any possibility of its being quickly opened from inside, it suddenly gave an inch.

She stepped back as if the whole heavy slab had been ripped aside and Grace Brown revealed, knife lifted high.

But, in an instant, she told herself not to act like a weak girl. Almost any door looking out on to the towpath might, with the rusting of the empty years, have become loosened.

She advanced again, put her shoulder to the rusty slab in front of her and pushed. Not another quarter-inch of movement.

On again. Each new door carefully checked. But at last the blind bridge came into sight through the drifting rain.

How long would it be necessary to keep up this to-and-fro march as far as the bridge and then back again to the start of the Canalside Walk? How many times over the same route? Three, four, half a dozen? At least she would allow herself no let-up until it was night dark.

The bridge.

Underneath it there was a thin patch of the path which the rain had not reached. She granted herself a short wait. Already the shoulders of her uniform jacket felt damp. How much longer, tramping in this wetting half-rain, before she was soaked through? What if she ended up catching a cold . . . Ridiculous. To abandon the fight with the madwoman Grace because of a few snuffles.

She stood there, half of her alert to a pitch of aware-ness, half of her lost in a fog of suppositions and doubts. It had been her intention to stay where she was under the bridge – it was not improbable that this would be the very place where Grace would come to her if she intended to speak before acting – for a precise ten minutes. She had even looked at her watch as she stepped into the shelter noting the exact time.

But, as the minutes went by and there was no sound

except the minuscule pattering of the now slightly harder rain, she became more and more prey to unaccustomed doubts.

Had it really been stupid not to have arranged for any sort of back-up? There were men and women in the Force highly skilled in street observation. One of them might after all have been able to keep her in view undiscovered by Grace. Or she could have had a radio on open channel easily concealed under her jacket. And then, if the sound of a struggle suddenly came to not-so-distant ears, muffled grunts, a half-cry, a plain shout, nearby officers could be on the scene within a minute or two, within seconds almost.

Thinking of the whole situation, wasn't it that she had chosen to behave, not like the hard detective she had earned the reputation of being, but like a silly new aide to CID risking all in a solitary bid to justify some ill-conceived theory of their own?

Had she . . .?

Startled into consciousness, not by some sudden surreptitious sound, but by the idiocy of the thoughts she had allowed to run repetitively on in her head, she looked rapidly all round, further along the canal towards Chapeltown from which Grace might only now be coming, across the murky water to the opposite bank, back behind to the grey mistiness of this towpath. Nothing. No one. Not a sound.

She looked at her watch.

Good God, twenty-two minutes vanished away.

About turn. Set off into the rain again. To hell with dampening shoulders. Ready on the instant for sudden attack, for a harshly croaking voice calling out *Top Cop, Top Cop?*

Tramp, tramp, tramp. Squelch, squelch.

And nothing ahead, only now plain signs of dusk under the dark grey, rain-oozing clouds. Another rat, this time scampering back into its lair under a high, grime-engrained wall.

Any other sound? Any give-away sound? Grace could, as she had envisaged earlier, have come here beforehand. She could have been watching, her crazed, glinting, marble-hard good eye at some crack in a wall somewhere, a quarter-inch gap between rust-brown metal door and slimed-wood doorpost, watching and noting. And now ready to come out. With the knife? With spitting incomprehensible words and curses?

Then, when it came, it was, despite all imaginings, almost entirely in an unexpected form.

The grey curtain of mist ahead, hardly lit by the very last of the daylight now, thickened to reveal a solid figure. And it was Grace Brown. There could be no mistaking her. Tall enough, thinly intense, a long greenish woollen dress clinging to her spare frame, much as her distant cousin, haystack-placid Mrs Studley, had described her arriving at the former police house at Westholme. And with, on her head, final proof if more proof were needed, a formless blue woollen hat.

Where had she come from? Obvious answer. From one of the places noted on the way to the blind bridge. A block, jammed against that rusty metal door, pulled away? A careful climb down from the crumbled wall, from any of the open-to-the-weather high windows? Less likely, but not impossible. Or, rake-thin as she seemed to be, standing legs apart, body leaning a little forward from the waist, had she been able to slide through that five-inch gap between the two huge ware-houses?

But no matter. Grace Brown was here. Materialized out of the soaking mist. A ghost. But a real ghost. A ghost intent on killing?

'I bin waiting fer you.'

Harriet paused for an instant, gathering herself up.

'Have you, Grace? So you know who I am?'

'Top Cop. Top Cop daring to come face-to-face with Cop Killer. That's who you are. An' that's what you're going to regret before long. You'll regret it all right.'

Harriet slipped her hand into the pocket of her dampened jacket, to feel with the tips of her fingers the solid weight of her illicit set of brass knuckles. Wrong, of course, to use them. But if she found herself at Grace's mercy . . . as well she might. Then one swift blow and the madwoman would lie unconscious on the grit-black path. And, once secured, even before summoning assistance on the mobile, splash, the heavy set of knuckles lost for ever in the muddy depths of the canal.

But, for the moment at least, there was no sign that the mist-shrouded figure some twenty yards off had in her hand the knife that had killed PC Titmuss and nearly been the end of PC Venning.

So knuckles stay where they are. Out of sight.

But approach. Softly. One step forward, and wait.

Squelch. The step taken.

Nineteen yards away now. Grace seemed not to

have taken in that step forward. Standing there silently and menacingly erect.

Another step. Taking more care than before to make the least possible noise. No movement from the distant, silent figure. One more step. Eighteen separating yards now. Less. And . . .

'Stay where you are. Yer don't think Grace Brown's just going to let herself be catched? Not till she's done all what she 'as to do, she ain't. And not after neither.'

'Why not, Grace?'

Try the soft soap, little chance though there was it would work. But if it gained another yard, another minute . . .

'Why not? Because of what you police done ter me. Killed my babby. Killed her 'fore she could see the light of day, the little pet. Oh, yes, they deserved to die, those police that done that. *Life for life*, that's what it says in the Good Book. An' a life for a life I took. That stupid copper, standing there a-puffing at 'is cigarette. An' that girl, no better than what she ought ter be from what I was hearing going about with me dishes in that canteen. She should of gone, too. It were right. *Eye for eye*. An' didn't I lose the sight of me eye when that fat sergeant o' police poked his elbow in me face? So that was right, too. That was what made me lose me babby, and it were right the foreigney girl should pay fer it.'

Despite that sharp *Stay where you are*, three sliding movements across the gritty, rain-soaked surface of the path had gone apparently unnoticed.

Time to put a reasoned view.

'But, Grace, even if it was right to have struck at those two, at PC Titmuss who had done nothing to you himself, at that girl Rukshana Syed you blinded and pushed to her death, even if those deaths were, in your eyes, right, were the rest of them? You should have stopped then, Grace. It wasn't right to go on. It wasn't right.'

'Grace knows what's right. Grace is right. You police were wrong. Grace is right.'

No use arguing there. The direct true course the only one.

'Grace Brown,' her voice clear and ringing over the still green water beside her as she stepped forward. 'I am arresting you on suspic—'

But the necessary, law-imposed phraseology blown away.

At the word *arresting* the statue-still figure in the mist was transformed in an instant to an oncoming, shouting, screaming, arms-whirling dervish. Rushing forward full-out.

'Whore of Babylon. Trick— Tricking . . .'

But Harriet, ready for just this, ducked sideways and then caught her by both her flailing arms.

No knife. So no need for anything more than the well-tested holds of the training school gym.

The face close up against her own. Sharp blue-button eyes, the right one seen now as unmoving, glazed. A spray of harsh spittle.

'I shouldn't ha' listened. Shouldn't have paid no heed to them posters. *Challenge – Top Cop – Challenge.*'

The writhing arms hard to hold.

Harriet swiftly changed her grip, brought her weight to bear fully down.

'But I won't be got. You ain't the one as . . . *Stripe for stripe*. I'll do it yet.'

A bony knee suddenly driven with full force into Harriet's stomach. A street fighter's trick. Unexpected.

Harriet heard the squeal of her own outforced breath. She heaved herself further forward, teeth gritted in a grimace of pain.

But there was no winning.

One more wild writhing motion, and Harriet felt the thin arms between her tightened fingers beginning to slip away. Another blow. This time, less well aimed and from the head in its blue woollen hat. But enough. Hard into the nose. And she fell.

Momentarily blinded by tears, she knew she had lost her. The knife. If Grace got out her killing knife she would be finished. And, flat on the ground, the brass knuckles, even if she could get them out quickly enough, useless.

Fool. Idiot.

In desperation she lashed out with her leg.

And felt it make contact. Saw Grace's long frame above her stagger.

She flung herself forwards into a half-upright crouch. For a moment they faced each other.

Grace, she saw, did have the knife in her hand now.

Knuckles.

In a moment they were round her right fist.

And Grace must, even with her single useful eye, have seen their gleam. And decided a struggle on equal terms was not for her.

The sound of scrambling, running feet.

Harriet stayed where she was just long enough to

suck in a single deep reviving breath, and set out in pursuit of the fleeing figure ahead, its arms held high, hands clawing the misty air, knife flashing. But she knew it would be touch and go. With every step she was having to fight back an urge to vomit. At every yard she gained she was unable to prevent herself swaying dangerously from side to side. At any moment – a half-felt fear jutted into her – she might find herself toppling into the cold, clammy waters down at her side.

But the mist-wreathed, wildly gesticulating figure ahead seemed to be making no better progress.

Sweat thick on her face, the blood from her nose salt in her half-open, air-sucking mouth, brass knuckles just thrust away banging awkwardly at her side, stomach pulsingly sore, on she ran.

Grace was within five yards of her now.

She breathed in great sucking gasps. Felt the tears in her eyes.

Yes. No, no.

As she swayed more wildly than ever, for an instant she seemed to see the water of the canal immediately beneath her. With a desperate lunge she flung herself inwards. A counter-sway outwards as she plunged on sent her back again within inches of the stone edge.

And arms came round her, firm, protective, obstructive.

She was brought to a full halt. She glimpsed Grace moving joggingly further and further away. Turned and saw whose firm arms had wrapped her round. Dr Smellyfeet's.

Chapter Eighteen

Grace Brown disappeared into the far mistiness. Dr Smellyfeet unwound his arms from Harriet. A ribby black cat emerged from a nearby tangle of dead willow-herb, regarded the pair of them with baleful eyes for a moment, erected its tail and stalked away.

'What the hell did you think you were doing?' Harriet demanded.

Dr Smellyfeet looked down at her through his drizzle-blurred glasses.

'I happened to be ringing you on a small matter,' he said, 'and, when your secretary told me you had gone out just saying you could be contacted in an emergency on your mobile, I put two and two together. Not difficult, actually.'

'And having made five, you came traipsing down here with the object of preventing me arresting Grace Brown. That it?'

Dr Smellyfeet pushed a large pink hand through the rain-damp tangle of his black curls.

'No,' he said. 'I don't think I did make five. I made four. I worked out, not only that you had gone to lay yourself open to attack from Grace, but where it was you would most likely be doing it. Somewhere near that tunnel bridge. I got to know this area pretty well, you know, when I was researching the Profile. All part of the picture.'

He achieved a twisted smile.

'And, if I may say so,' he added, 'it was a good job I did come down here. Or at this minute you'd very likely be trying to haul yourself up on to dry land here.'

Harriet looked down at the canal's now black-as-night water.

'All right, yes, you may have saved me from going in there. But on the other hand very probably I'd have saved myself. And then at this minute, as you put it, I could be arresting that seven-times murderer.'

'Six, actually. Your PC Venning hasn't died. In fact, that's what I was ringing you about. I'd been on to the hospital. Where they told me, incidentally, that you hadn't enquired after him.'

'No, I hadn't. You may think I'm a hard bitch, and perhaps I am, but I didn't see there was any point in doing the all-pals-together, sentimental thing. If he does die, they'll be quick enough to tell me.'

'Okay, I suppose. But, as a matter of fact, he's out of intensive care now and recovering well.'

'I'm glad to hear it. I really am, if you must know. Why should I wish the fellow any harm? He's a useful copper, so Rob Roberts told me on the phone when he'd looked him up in his precious files. Which I did ask him to do, see if he had a wife, kids.'

'Yes, well, okay. Still, I'm glad in any case I did come here. All right, you might have managed to save yourself going over the edge there, but from the way you were swaying as you ran I'm not so sure you would have done. And there's another thing . . .'

'What?'

He gave her an assessing look before speaking.

'This: if you had caught up with Grace, and if I hadn't been here, what, as a matter of interest, would you have done?'

'I'd have arrested her, of course.'

'And treated her properly? She's a human being like the rest of us, you know.'

The thought of the brass knuckles still weighting her jacket pocket came briefly into Harriet's mind. And the added thought of what she had resolved to do if mad Grace had proved to be the better fighter: the splash as the heavy knobbed strip of brass went into the canal.

'As far as I'm concerned,' she said, looking Dr Smellyfeet straight in the eye, 'Grace Brown is a law-breaker, a six-times – right, six times – murderer and as such it's my duty as a police officer to arrest her when-ever and wherever she is to be found.'

'Oh, I don't question that. But what I have wondered, if only at the back of my mind while I've been collaborating with you on her case, is what sort of treatment Grace was going to get when she came into police hands.'

'Have you never read the Police and Criminal Evidence Act, 1984? You should have done if you were going to go poking your nose into murder investi-gations. It happens to lay down very stringent provisions about the handling of suspects under arrest. Too stringent, perhaps. But the provisions are there, and it is as much my duty to abide by them as it is my duty to effect an arrest in the first place.'

'Oh, yes, I have read the Act, and I do know what a police officer is supposed to do. But I sometimes have my suspicions that corners get cut and regulations even boldly flouted. Not by every police officer, but frankly sometimes by those with a reputation for wanting to *stop the rot* by whatever means they can.'

'And I, let me tell you, sometimes have my suspicions about people who are not police officers, who are not – I was talking about this at my press conference just this morning – engaged in the state of war that exists between the forces of law and the forces of criminal disruption. Aren't they— Aren't you, Peter Scholl, too damn soft? Aren't you one of the people who believe fundamentally that the world's a nice place? Against all the actual evidence, don't you, consciously or not, deny that there are people who are not nice? You still hope that somehow deep down everybody is good. Well, I know different. I know that there are people about who are a hundred per cent self-centred. Who believe they've some sort of right to do just what pleases them, whether it's to seize hold of anything they take a fancy to, provided it's not being clutched tight by someone bigger than themselves, or whether it's sticking a knife into someone they take a dislike to. Such people exist. And they've got to be checked. By using tougher tactics than they can rise to. I know it's an unpopular view. I know what most people want is to have a nice, easy, comfortable world. But they can't.'

She paused for breath, cursing herself for, in her vulnerable state, saying more than she had meant to.

'Oh, yes,' she went on however, 'and there are moments when I'd like to believe the world's like that myself. It would make life a lot easier if it truly was and I could act as if it was. But it isn't. It is a foul and nasty place, despite the bits here and there that are different, good, nice. But, while I know there are a hundred per cent selfish shits in existence, then I know it's my task, like it or not, to put my foot down on them hard.'

But at last she managed to regain the sense of proper behaviour that under the stress she had undergone had deserted her.

'Right, I can't stay here arguing,' she barked out. 'I've been head-butted by that damn woman. I've been kicked in the stomach by her. And I got soaked marching up and down here waiting for her. So I need to get home. Goodbye.'

'But, Harriet, are you all right to be left on your own? Shouldn't I be seeing you home?'

'No.'

She waited there, deliberately declining to move, despite the shivering fit she had not succeeded in staving off, till Dr Smellyfeet at last went tramping back in the direction of the blind bridge. And, when she was sure he was out of hearing, she slipped the brass knuckles from her pocket and slid, rather than threw, the heavy metal strip into the canal. There was hardly a splash as it disappeared beneath the water.

All over. And out of it not too badly.

But, although she drove all the way to her house without too much strain, as she stepped up on to the orch veranda she did for a moment have to clutch at its sturdy railing to prevent herself from falling.

*

212

'Are you all right?' Marjorie spluttered excitedly, as Harriet came into her office next morning. 'You've got a terribly bruised nose.' Luckily her impromptu murmur about 'walking into a door' was interrupted by a ring on her phone. She picked it up.

'Harriet, are you all right?' Dr Smellyfeet.

'Peter.' She drew in a long breath. 'It's kind of you to enquire. But, yes, I am okay. Nothing worse than some damage to my nose that's given my secretary an excuse for girlish palpitations.'

'Well, I'm glad to hear. Not about the palpitations. But about you. Look, I'm sorry I said what I did when I did last evening, I should have thought. It was hardly the time to produce the sort of arguments I did. But . . .'

'I think I gave as good as I got. Said more than I meant, actually. So forget about it, yes?'

'Well, okay. But there is something else I do want to say about Grace.'

'Yes?'

'About what she's likely to do now.'

'As a matter of fact, I thought while I was getting dressed this morning that I ought to ask for your opinion on that. What is she likely to do? How will she have reacted to yesterday? She felt she'd been tricked, you know. That I hadn't really been seeking a confrontation. More, that I'd arranged a trap. She must be blaming herself for having let herself alter course.'

'Yes, you're right. She'll see herself, I believe, as weak in having been deflected from what she sees as the right and only way she must go.'

'Yes, she said as much down there at the canal. In so far as she was making sense at all.'

'So, well, the first thing to realize is that she'll be back more rigidly than ever to wanting to give out *stripe for stripe*.'

'And how, from your reading of her, do you think she's going to go about that?'

'Look, Harriet, I'm not a clinical psychiatrist. I don't specialize in aberrant human behaviour. I haven't the qualifications.'

'Okay, okay, I know all that. But I have come to have some sort of trust in you. And I want to know what your informed guess is. Damn it, you've been thinking about the wretched woman for weeks now. You must have some ideas.'

'Well, I have. But you're not to take whatever I say for gospel.'

'No, no. You're all ready to back down at the slightest indication you may be wrong. We'll take that as read. Now, what do you think?'

'Thanks for your confidence.'

'Peter, what do you think? I asked. I want to know.'

'Well then, I'll go out on a bit of a limb. I'll bet – I gather at your briefing yesterday you had all the sex shops in Birchester asked to report any out-of-the-way sales of whips – well, I'll bet that a report comes in before this day's out. Or, well, by tomorrow at the latest.'

'That's what I like: someone who's definite in his opinions.'

'I'm sorry. But this isn't something I like doing. If I told you that Grace is even now putting finishing touches – obsessively going over and over every detail – of her plan to kill some Greater Birchester Police officer by somehow using a whip, that would be fair enough. We've known that in essence for weeks. But to go on, to go further, would be almost total guesswork. I mean, I could say that her likeliest target is you. You. The now doubly hated figure. But, as I say, it would be guesswork. I can't give you any sort of worthwhile analysis without having gathered the facts. And then having compared them with what I've learnt already.'

'And in the meantime Grace Brown will have murdered another police officer, and then gone and done what? Committed suicide? Gone into hiding down in London, or somewhere where most likely she'll never be found? Anyhow, escaped justice.'

'That's the sort of attitude I was on about yesterday. I know you feel you're justified, and I accepted a great deal of your arguments then. But you really ought to try to see things from a wider point of view. It isn't all about justice all the time, for heaven's sake.'

'Look, Peter. In my book it is. It is about justice. There are people out there who are doing wrong. I don't care whether it's as much wrong as Grace Brown has done, or as much wrong as someone does who puts a brick through a car window for fun. They're doing wrong. And I'm there, as a police officer, to stop them. And that's all there is to it.'

Dr Smellyfeet's bet almost came off. It was during the next morning but one, only hours after the latest time he had fixed on, that a report of the sale of a whip landed on Harriet's desk in the Incident Room. There had, it said, been a call from the *All You Want To Know* sex shop, saying that an old lady *looking like she was a scarecrow off of a farm* had prowled round for five or ten minutes – *no other customers in so early, thank Gawd* – and, with a twenty-pound note pulled from inside the front of her dress, had bought a whip. Questioned, the shop manager, after hastily saying the whip was *only a fun thing, you know, I mean people are entitled to play games if they want, ain't they?*, had described her purchase as being some five-feet long and made from plaited strips of black leather.

Harriet, passing this on to the detectives present, silenced the guffawing laughter it evoked.

'No, not a fun thing. Something that could be, in the hands of Grace Brown, plainly dangerous.'

'So what do we do now, ma'am?' DI Coleman asked, anxiety not altogether kept out of his voice.

'We do not let that woman flog any member of Greater Birchester Police.'

From the officers sitting round there came a sound which was not quite a disbelieving *How?*, but not far from it.

'You'll tell me we didn't succeed in protecting Cadet Chatterton,' Harriet snapped. 'You'll tell me former Greater Birchester Police officer George Studley wasn't kept out of that madwoman's clutches either. And there I'll say *How could we know he at least was in any sort of danger?* But I won't make any excuses over the death in that blazing house of PC Strachan. We knew some sort of *burning for burning* death was being planned. We failed to prevent it. I failed to prevent it. I dare say you all know that PC Venning is now expected to make a total recovery. I'm glad of it. But I'm unrepentant about putting him into such danger as I did. A police officer has to risk his or her life on occasion. And with PC Venning, to an extent, we did not fail. We forced Grace Brown to take a real risk, and in doing so at least she lost her hiding-place.'

She waited then for a moment for this to sink in.

Should she say anything about the chance she had deliberately given Grace yesterday at the canal? Had what had happened down there become common knowledge, at least among the officers there in front of her? All right, she had fended off enquiries about her bruised nose, and Peter Scholl could be trusted not to go talking about it, but some patrolling constable might have seen something and gossiped.

But, no. There was silence in the big room. Her failure to hold Grace still a matter that need never be known about. So, no reference to it.

'Right. DI Coleman has asked what's to be done to protect every member of the Force from a possibly deadly assault by a whip-wielding fanatic of a woman. And my answer is: nothing.'

A stir from the intent hearers.

'Yes, nothing. Think. What could I do? What could anyone realistically do? Wrap each member of the Force in protective sheeting? Issue guns all round? No. The initiative, for better or worse, is with that woman with her whip. But, to use it, she has to take risks, big risks. And that's when we'll get her. So it's a question of total alertness. But it's not just – all right, this is a pun – your own back you've got to watch. You've got to watch the officer who Grace Brown makes her target. And get to Grace before she gets to them.'

She saw glances go from one of her hearers to another.

It was working. Despite the long period they had been engaged in the sterile hunt, they were now – it was easy to see – reanimated. If Grace came into the open she would be caught, if it was humanly possible.

'And all that doesn't mean to say,' she went on, 'we won't continue actively to hunt that woman. I'm still pretty sure she's hiding somewhere in the Chapeltown area, and incidentally Dr Scholl, whose advice I respect, confirms that. We almost got her moving her hiding-place after her attack on PC Venning when in DI Johnston's immortal words *the bird had flown.*'

A titter of nervous laughter.

Which evidently served to irritate Johnston.

He jumped to his feet at the back of the room.

'There is another thing, ma'am,' he said, something like a glare on his face. 'I don't know if you want this mentioned. But I definitely think it ought to be.'

Has he, after all, heard some canteen gossip about the notorious Hard Detective being seen staggering away from the canal with blood on her face?

'Spit it out, DI. I don't want any festering anywhere in my team.'

The glare increased.

'Very well, ma'am. It's this. There's been a lot in the papers, in that rag the *Evening Star,* about you issuing a direct challenge to the woman they're always calling Cop Killer. When I was down in Chapeltown with my searchers the day after you could hardly see the place for newspaper bills.'

'Hardly my responsibility, DI.'

218

'No, ma'am. I'm well aware of that. But what I want to know is: what are you doing about it? Are you deliberately walking the streets hoping Grace Brown will come running? Or are you ignoring the whole stupid business, and staying inside the building here where you're well safe?'

'What do you expect me to do, DI?'

A look of something like astonishment at this turn-about, in so far as the Scotsman would allow it.

'Well?'

'I dinna ken, ma'am. I suppose if you did present yourself where she's likely to find you, it could bring her to the fore. Of course, you'd have to have good back-up. I'd be happy to oblige myself, ma'am, if that was the way of it.'

'Thank you, DI. And if we do have to resort to some strategy of that sort, and it may come to that, I'll certainly take your offer up.'

But now DI Coleman joined in.

'All the same, ma'am,' he said, 'isn't it possible Grace will try to take up this so-called challenge? If she's looking for an officer to use that whip on, then – begging your pardon, ma'am – wouldn't you be her likeliest choice?'

'Yes, DI. Yes, I suppose I would be.' After yesterday. Yes, Grace may very well target me. 'And she's welcome to try.'

'Well, then, ma'am, shouldn't you have back-up, as DI Johnston's suggested? I mean, you are in all probability at considerable risk. We don't know how much that woman may know about you, about what your routines are, about where outside of here you can be found. After all, she worked in the canteen at Queen Street, we know that, and there'll have been bits of gossip said there about you. You know what a canteen's like.'

'Yes, DI. I do remember what a canteen's like. And thank you for your kindly thoughts. But I like to think I can look after myself, you know.' For an instant she saw Grace Brown rushing towards her out of the mist the day before. 'And I do always carry a mobile phone. So I don't think we need concern ourselves too deeply with that particular prospect.'

She took one more look round the intent faces in the room.

'So let me remind you all that Grace may well be moving from place to place down in Chapeltown. Don't go thinking that just because one possible hideyhole's been searched she may not use it again. She's a planner. Dr Scholl has proved that to me. To the hilt. She's perfectly capable of working out where our searches have been and how she can outwit us. But don't let her. We're going to be the ones doing the outwitting. Get to it.'

Chapter Nineteen

Approaching home that evening, Harriet, paradoxically exhausted after a day with nothing happening bar the report on Grace buying the whip, no other sighting of her, no report of any attack, could not but acknowledge she was, to a ridiculous extent, prey to fears and alarms. Perhaps DI Johnston's criticisms got under my skin, she thought. That offer of personal protection rankled. Yes, a little.

Or is the need to keep secret that stupid, unsuccessful encounter with Grace somehow undermining me still? Do I really need to conceal at all costs what happened? Aren't I too concerned about my own status? The Hard Detective worsted? Ashamed of that? And, to add to that humiliation, the Hard Detective so battered by an elderly madwoman that she was unable even to run in a straight line. And at last had to be saved from a ducking in the canal.

But perhaps the fears scuttling round in my mind were put there by the real concern DI Coleman showed. Yet was he right to be concerned? Am I really in danger? More now than when I got Tim Patterson to issue my challenge? Actually in worse danger than I was down at the canal on my own, only my knuckle-duster as protection?

She gave herself a stiffer than usual whisky and ginger.

A jolt of alcohol and back to normality? But nothing happened. She simply sat brooding.

Have I been tasked with a job that's beyond me? Is being a hard police officer, as I've prided myself on being, not enough faced with a truly hard task? But what more could I have done? What more, be honest, would any detective in the Greater Birchester Police have done? Nothing. And I did something more. None of them would have contrived that challenge.

But how clever had that actually been? It had gone wrong. Yet it needn't have done. If Grace's knee hadn't landed at just the right place by chance, by sheer chance, I'd have had her safely in a cell now. Even if I hadn't swerved so precariously at just the moment that Dr Smellyfeet – no, that Peter Scholl – was coming up behind me, I could very well have caught up with Grace.

Yes, but it did go wrong. All right, it may turn out yet that we hunt Grace down when she comes out to use that whip. But the whole business of my challenge went disastrously wrong. No getting past that.

God, the truth is I'd love to have John here at the moment. Here and not in damn, distant Brazil. To lay it all out to him. Okay, he'd do no more than reassure me, tell me I'm doing my best. Even if the twins were here, I'd break a resolution at this moment and tell them about it all. And they'd probably try to reassure me, too. *Mum, hey, you're the Top Cop.* I wouldn't believe them. I wouldn't believe John. But I could snuggle those words to me. And feel better.

But I don't feel better. I know my challenge to Grace Brown did go disastrously wrong. So is it that I wasn't right in the first place to trick sharp Tim Patterson into issuing my challenge for me? Have I . . . The thought grew, try how she might to force it down. Have I been too sure I was right all along? From the best of the *Stop the Rot* days even? When in Tim Patterson's office they called me Miss Eyemright. Miss I'm right. Yes, that went home. I refused to let myself think about it when he brought it out there in the Gardens. Rejected it. Pushed it away. But now . . . Now, don't I have to look at it fairly and squarely? Miss Eyemright. Am I that? Right every time about everything?

A long hard mental inward look.

And, no. No, truly I don't think of myself as being right about everything. But I am right in my whole attitude to the wrong in my world. I am right to be the Hard Detective.

Yes.

She glanced at her watch.

Hell, the time. Should have been getting some supper together half an hour ago. Missed the eight o'clock radio news. Suppose, if there'd been any development I'd have been told. But all the same . . .

She heaved herself out of her chair and strode into the kitchen.

A ready-meal from the freezer. Once again.

Carrying a tray through the hall, heading for the sitting room – supper on my knee, soothing burble of the telly, early bed – the scream that rang out seemed almost to come from inside the house.

For an instant she froze.

Teenagers larking about? No. That sound I know well enough. I've marched up often enough and put an end to it. No, that was the scream of real fright. Fear? It might be. Yes.

She stooped, put the tray down on the carpet.

Another scream rang out. And another. Someone out there in the road, or even inside the gate screaming in fear. Almost certainly. So, deal with it.

She went to the door, quietly wound back the security bolt.

Then a thought.

Grace Brown. Could the screamer be her? Could it be a planned trick to get her hated enemy out into the open? But Grace wouldn't find her way here. Nobody knew where Detective Superintendent Martens lived. Or hardly anybody outside those in the Force who needed to know. That had been half the point of not using the married name. To keep Miss Martens and Mrs Piddock as far apart as possible. All right, it hadn't always worked. When the small-time criminals in the B Division had been riled enough by *Stop the Rot* some of them had managed to track DCI Martens back to her home – and put their parcels of shit through the letter-box.

But Grace Brown, the Bible quoter who had driven her cousins the Studleys half-crazy with *prayers before, prayers after and as many as could be fitted in between*, she would never have mixed with that sort of low-life. So she could not possibly—

Another thought. Bursting in like an unwelcome stranger. Grace Brown, the canteen worker, collecting dirty dishes and keeping her ears open. And one day at least Rob Roberts, trying perhaps to earn acceptance from the macho constables who laughed at him and his precious files, telling them her real name was Piddock. The guffaws and the jokes.

So Grace could know my married name. But what good would that do her? Rob Roberts wouldn't have gone about yakking out my address. So how could she know this is where I live? All right, there is, as a matter of fact, only one *Piddock* in the Birchester phone book. But how likely is it that Grace, hiding in derelict houses, sleeping rough somewhere in Chapeltown, would be able to consult a phone book? She couldn't exactly take one from some neat shelf under a telephone table in her nice, comfortable home. And it's been many years since a telephone directory was placed in every phone box. The sort of vandals *Stop the Rot* was put into operation to check saw to that. So, really there's nowhere for Grace to look up this address.

But if somehow . . .?

The knuckleduster. Get it.

No, deep in the mud of the canal.

So, fail to fall for the trick? If it is a trick . . . But if it's really some girl in real distress? Rape? A brutal beating? Then only one thing to do. Go out.

And, right, if there's no girl there, no rapist. If it is Grace . . . Then still go out. Tackle her. Face her again. Tackle her, even if the advantage this time must be with the one who's laid the trap.

Call for back-up first? The mobile's here on the hall

table. Is there time? If I don't respond to that scream as quickly as I would if I'd never thought of Grace, she'll know I've seen through her trick, and— And, as likely as not, she'll just creep away into the dark. Peter's planner.

Right. Fling door wide.

The blank emptiness of the night. Pause for a moment. What I would do, truly responding to a scream of fear? Call out? Yes.

'Who's there?'

Silence. The warmth of an April night. The almond tree faintly scenting the air, damp from the last shower. A glimmer of daffodils down by the garden wall.

'Anyone there?'

That should be enough. Enough for Grace to believe her trick's worked. And now it's all but certain it is a trick. A girl, even locked tight under a man's pressing body, must have managed some squeak of a call for help.

So, next move?

Step out. Step on to the veranda, grasp the rail, peer forwards.

And Grace? Where will she be? What's the next move she's planned? Down there in the shadow of the wall? She could be there, all right. If she's managed to get herself some dark garment, she could be crouching there, totally invisible with that distant street lamp making the shadow even denser.

Wait. If there's a patch where the daffodils are not to be seen, that could be her blocking them out, crushing them. Or, no, it could just be that no flowerhead happens to catch the light coming from the door here.

All right. If I was going to the rescue of a screaming girl, I'd go cautiously. So now do no more than lean well out into the darkness to look from side to side? Call out once again? Yes. Why not?

'Who's there? Is there anybo—'

The sudden heavy blow on the back of the neck. The just grasped realization that a body – Grace's body – had tumbled from the porch roof above. Clawing hands at her hair, face, arms. Tugging sharply.

And the consciousness, even as it happened, that the trick Grace had played had worked.

That she was tumbling forward, falling to the ground in front of the veranda. Helpless. That thin wiry gangling body all over her.

So, roll.

Putting every ounce of effort into it, fighting against the dizziness in her head, Harriet rolled across the soft earth of the narrow flowerbed bordering the veranda on to the path, the sharpness of the edging tiles momentarily halting her, then digging painfully into her side.

But in a moment she knew she had done it. The netting limbs that had pinned her down were no longer there.

She was lying flat on her back.

She looked desperately from side to side. Where was Grace? What was she preparing to do now?

Then she made it out. In the darkness, all the deeper for the swath of light still coming fruitlessly from the open house door, she could see Grace's body jerking limb by limb into an upright position. Did she know where her target was? She must do.

Up. Get up. Level the terms.

She forced herself on to her knees, keeping Grace firmly in sight at every instant.

And then she realized what the half-silhouetted figure in front of her was doing. Raising her arm. And dangling from it, just visible, the whip.

Lunge at her. Get to the feet and lunge. Before she has time to—

Too late. Too late. Her arm swinging down andforwards. Left arm. Left-handed Grace. Girl at Boots said.

So dodge left, me.

Crack.

Searing pain slashed across Harriet's face as she fell backwards. For one instant everything was blotted out. But for one instant only. Then she realized the whip stroke had landed high. Across her forehead.

But she was down. Down. Limp on her side, and at the mercy of the woman dedicated to killing police officers. Might be dead already.

Now. Now it had come. The final moment. The end.

'Stop!'

Harriet heard the shout. She was unable to make out whether it was hallucination, or if she'd really heard a loud male voice shouting *Stop!* from somewhere in the road outside.

But Grace, she saw, as she looked up through half-closed, defensive eyelids, had had no doubts. Turning like a spitting cat, she was glaring into the darkness.

'No,' she yelled out now. 'You're too late. Too late. I've won. I've won. *Stripe for stripe* I've killed her. Killed her, killed.'

Then she darted away. In through the open house

door. Which slammed. A noise like a reverberating gunshot. And an extra shade of darkness descending on the garden.

'Harriet. Mrs Piddock. Are you— Are you all right?' Who . . .?

She managed to lift up her head a little. Her vision swam, cleared.

A mop of fair hair, almost white in the darkness. A face almost black, but ruddy, bending over her. And a big fluffy moustache.

Rob Roberts.

'What— What you here?'

'You're okay then? Er— ma'am?'

'What are you doing here, I asked.'

'I— er— Well, it's a long story. But are you all right? I mean, are you?'

'I'm as well as can be expected,' she said, unable to stop herself retreating into her foetal position. 'And please answer my question.'

'It— It was like this. I was worried about you. Not— Not tonight. But when I thought about that challenge the paper said you'd made. And— And, well, I wondered how you'd go about it. Would you have someone to guard your back? Only I knew you wouldn't want that. So I—'

'Get on with it, man.'

Harriet felt vigour returning. And the pain across her forehead beating out at double, triple strength.

'Yes. Yes, ma'am. So . . . Well, I sort of guessed you might go down to that deserted stretch of the canal running along from Chapeltown. So . . . So I just went down there. Only, because I'd left it too long, what I

saw was you coming away to where you'd left your car.
And your face was all bloody. So I followed you back
here and saw you'd got indoors all right, then I worked
out you must have met Grace Brown, and— And, well
come off worst.'

'What I asked was: why are you here? Now?'

She still felt incapable of moving.

'Yes. Yes, sorry. It was— Well, the same thing really.
I mean, I thought— I wondered what Grace Brown
would do now that she'd met you, as it were face to face.
And I knew her next thing was *stripe for stripe*, and I
worried she might have a go at you like that. I mean,
she's killed. Time and again. So, well, I was sitting there
at home – my wife's left me, did I tell you that? – and I
was thinking about you. And Grace Brown. And . . . and
everything. And I thought I must just pop round to the
house here, see if you seemed to be all right. And, well,
I suppose I came just in the nick of time.'

Harriet mentally roused herself.

'Yes, Rob,' she said, lying huddled there. 'Yes, you
did arrive in the nick of time. And, yes, I'm grateful.
Very grateful. If you hadn't shouted out when you did
that woman would have looked at me more carefully.
And found I wasn't dead. And then I soon should've
been. No doubt about that.'

'But do you think . . . I mean, has she just run
through the house there and got away? Or . . .'

'Or, as you say, Rob. Or has she been foxed by the
locked back-door, the key well hidden away? And
the windows with safety-locks on as well? She most
likely has. So what's she doing— Rob, your car's here?
You've got a phone?'

'Yes. Yes, I had it—'

'Then for God's sake, call this in. I want the house surrounded. I want the firearms team, John's shotgun's in there, locked away but . . . I want them now.'

'Ma'am. Yes, ma'am.'

Rob scuttled off.

Harriet decided to lie where she was. Grace might well look out of a window, if she still was trapped in the house, and if she did not see her victim on the ground there, she would come out again. And – the thought forced its way inside the throbbing pain in her face – *I'm in no state to get her on my own.*

The not-so Hard Detective. Well, hard detectives and soft, we're all human. At the mercy sometimes of brute facts. Not always up on top.

Chapter Twenty

Soon, faster than might have been expected, there came the multiple screeching of brakes, running feet, orders echoing decisively across the night air. Harriet staggered to her feet. Saw the faithful Rob standing discreetly just inside the garden gate. And then a moment later saw someone she had not expected. Dr Smellyfeet.

Frowning, she walked towards him.

Rob, as if guessing, even fearing, what she might be going to say, came forward.

'Ma'am. Ma'am, I thought it might be a good idea to let Dr Scholl know. I mean, I thought his advice . . .'

'You did quite right, Inspector,' Dr Smellyfeet said, loudly and clearly.

Harriet stopped.

'I dare say you could be useful, Peter. But just at the moment I'm more concerned with making sure that woman doesn't get out of the house. If she hasn't found where I hide the back-door key, or contrived to unlock a window.'

DI Coleman had responded to Rob's call, and Harriet went over to him and, brushing aside his enquiries about the deep weal across her forehead, began making arrangements for a siege. She had hardly been talking for five minutes when one of the constables Coleman had sent to the back of the house came trotting up.

'She's in there all right, sir. We've seen her shadow through the blind in what looks like the kitchen.'

'Yes,' Harriet said. 'She could well be there.'

'Well then, ma'am,' Coleman asked. 'Now we know we've got her nicely bottled up, what are we going to do?'

'Leave her for a bit, DI. See if she makes any sort of move. Don't hesitate to let the chaps show themselves. We want to put as much pressure on as possible. With any luck, she'll try to make a break for it. Unless she has managed to get hold of my husband's shotgun, she isn't armed. Except for that whip. So we shouldn't have too much trouble making an arrest. Or she may want to talk, and then we'll coax or trick her to where we can get her.'

'Do I stand down the firearms boys, then?'

'No. No, I don't think so. If the worst comes to the worst and one of our side's in danger, a shot might finish things nicely.'

From the darkness outside the glaring lights, by now showing up every brick, every piece of woodwork of the house, a voice came.

Dr Smellyfeet's.

'Harriet. Miss Martens, can I have a word? Urgently.'

'Yes. Yes, I suppose so. You happy, DI?'

'Ma'am.'

'Right then, Doctor, what is it?'

233

Dr Scholl kept his voice down.

'Listen, Harriet, I heard that. You aren't going to arrange to have Grace shot?'

Harriet looked at him.

'If I have to, I will. I carry the rank to order firearms officers to use their weapons if a suspect has a gun.'

'No, I asked if what you were going to do was to arrange one of those incidents that have happened in the past.'

'No. No, I suppose I'm not. I don't want an interminable inquiry afterwards. And the possibility of it going against me. So, no, Peter, I'm not going to play dirty. But if one of my team is in danger . . . And let me remind you the woman in the house there has not hesitated to kill police officers. If another of them is in real danger now, I'll happily take full responsibility for anything that happens.'

'Full responsibility for the death of a human being? A human being who's beyond knowing what she's doing?'

'A human being, as I've just pointed out to you, who has killed six other human beings. Who's broken the law at its most serious. No, Peter, I happen to think she deserves to die. But I know, too, it's not my duty to see her killed. But it is my duty to arrest her, and that's what I'm going—'

An upper window in the house was thrust open with such force that every single person's attention switched to it like the clicked points of a rail line. And to the gaunt figure just inside.

'You know what, Peter?' Harriet murmured. 'I'd like to take one single shot at her now.'

'Harriet, she's a hopeless, disoriented person. Have some compassion, for God's sake.'

Any reply she might have made was cut short by a screeching voice from above.

'You police devils. Killing my babby. Killing the poor mite unborn. Police. Police. But I've had my way. I've done what was to be done. I've taken a life for a life. I've taken an eye for an eye. A tooth for a tooth. Hand for hand. Foot for foot. Burning for burning. Wound for wound. I've killed them all. And now I've killed the last of them. The Top Cop. Thought she'd hidden herself away from me. But I traced her. I tracked her. I heard her true name. I went to the big Post Office and looked in the phone book. I found where Mrs Piddock lived. And *stripe for stripe* I've killed her. So I'm going now. Going to the blessed land. Going where there's peace. Peace.'

And then Harriet stepped forward into the ring of light round the house.

'No, Grace Brown,' she shouted up.

A violent throb of pain ran down her face from the muscular movement she had made in calling out.

She ignored it.

'No, Grace Brown, I'm still alive. Your trick wasn't good enough. I'm alive, Grace Brown, and I'm coming to take you in.'

She turned and went over to the wall between her house and the next at a spot just where the almond tree grew. She stooped, scraped away the rain-sticky earth in the narrow flower-bed there, came up with an old Ovaltine tin, prised off its top and poured into her outstretched palm the spare set of keys to the house.

'Harriet,' Peter Scholl said, as he saw what she had got. 'Harriet, let her do it. Let her use that shotgun and end her life. Get the peace she craves.'

'No, Peter. A murderer is there inside. I am going to effect an arrest. No criminal is going to get away unpunished so long as I have anything to do with it.'

She went over to the house door and opened it. DI Coleman and one of the armed officers came up close behind her. Quickly she went over to the stairs and quietly went up them, neither delaying nor hurrying.

At the top she went straight across the landing. The door of the front bedroom was just open. She pushed it wide.

Grace Brown had turned away from the window. For a moment Harriet's eyes went to the long black snaking whip lying on the bedspread.

Then she spoke.

'Grace Brown, I am arresting you on suspicion of murdering Police Constable Titmuss, Woman Police Constable Syed, Detective Superintendent Froggott, Police Cadet Chatterton, former Police Constable Studley, and Police Constable Strachan. You do not have to say anything. But it may harm your defence if you do not mention when questioned something which you later rely on in court. Anything you do say may be given in evidence.'